SOPHENE

Published by Sophene 2019

Spanish Tales was first published in 2019 by Sophene Pty Ltd.

These tales were originally translated to the English language by
J. Munoz Escamez and Elsie Spicer Eels.

www.sophenebooks.com

ISBN-13: 978-1-925937-23-7

SPANISH TALES

A COLLECTION OF CLASSIC SPANISH FOLK TALES

SPANISH TALES

A COLLECTION OF CLASSIC SPANISH FOLK TALES

CONTENTS

THE CITY OF FORTUNE

Once upon a time there was a boy named Rupert, who was the sharpest and most prudent boy in his village, and indeed in any of those to be found for twenty leagues[1] around.

One night he was with a group of boys of his own age, who, gathered round the fire, were listening with amazement to a veteran soldier, covered with scars, which had gained him the modest stripes of a sergeant pensioner, and who was telling the story of his adventures. The narrator was at the most interesting point of his tale.

"The great City of Fortune," he said, "is situated on the summit of a very high mountain, so steep that only very few have succeeded in reaching the top. There gold circulates in such abundance that the inhabitants do not know what to do with the precious metal. Houses are built of it, the walls of the fortress are of solid silver, and the cannons that defend it are enormous pierced diamonds. The streets are paved with *duros*[2], always new, because as soon as they begin to lose their brilliance they are replaced by others just minted.

"You ought to see the cleanliness of it! The dirt is pure gold dust, which the dust carts collect in order to throw in large baskets into the drains.

"The pebbles against which we stumble continually are brilliants as large as nuts, despised on account of the extraordinary abundance with which the soil supplies them. In a word, he who lives there may consider the most powerful of the earth as beggars.

"The worst of it is that the path which leads there is

1   A league is an old measure of distances, approximately the same as three miles.

2   A duro was a Spanish silver dollar.

rough and difficult, and most people succumb without having been able to arrive at the city of gold."

Rupert did not let the words of the soldier go in at one ear and out at the other; and so it was that, hardly had the occasion of being alone with him arisen before he inquired:

"Do you know the way to this enchanted city?"

"I should rather think so, my son; but I do not advise you to try the journey."

"Why?"

"The way is long and rocky. I came back the first day, startled at the difficulties which must be overcome. But anyhow, if you are resolved to go, I must give you the following warning. In order to get to Fortune there are two paths: a very broad one, full of stones and crags; if you go that way the sharp points of the pebbles will tear your feet to pieces and you will be crushed by fatigue. A thousand terrible difficulties will arise to meet you; you will have to struggle with cruel enemies, and if, at last, you succeed in vanquishing all, you will arrive at Fortune already old and worn, when riches will be of no use to you. The other path is level and short, but..."

"Enough! Do not say any more; show me it now, and I will look after the rest."

"All right, all right! I will show it to you, and God grant that your not having wished to hear me to the end will not bring you suffering."

And the little rogue, without saying good-bye to his parents or his brother, began to walk in the direction the old soldier had shown him; and went on and on, happier than a sandboy, thinking of the riches which awaited him, and which he already believed to have within reach of his hand.

At the end of two days he arrived at the bank of a large

river. On it was a boat, and in the boat a negro of colossal stature.

Our lad approached the boatmen and asked him:

"Good man, is this the way to Fortune?"

"Yes, little boy, but it is necessary to cross the river."

"Good, then take me across."

"Do you know how much it costs?"

"No."

"Fifty duros."

"But do I look as if I had them, or had even seen them in my life? Be kind and take me over for nothing."

"This river, my little friend, is never crossed for free. It is the first step towards Fortune and it must be paid for somehow. If you have no money, never mind; let me cut off a little piece of your heart. Perhaps it will hurt you a bit at first, but later you will feel as if you were whole."

Rupert allowed the man to open his chest and to take out a piece of his heart. When he crossed to the other side he gave a sigh of satisfaction. The first step was taken, and he already saw the beautiful City of Fortune, whose resplendent walls sent out lovely reflections. But he noticed that he was much less anxious to arrive at the city of gold and had a strange emptiness in his chest. He continued his walk; but he had not taken a hundred steps when a new difficulty arose to obstruct the way. This stretched between two inaccessible mountains and the entrance to the defile was kept by another guardian as black as the one of the boat.

"Where are you going, boy?" he asked our lad.

"To the City of Fortune."

"Quite so, this is the way; but you have to pay for the passage. The payment is a little piece of heart."

Without hesitating, Rupert opened his chest and left a handful of fibres of that organ of life in the hands of the terrible gatekeeper.

And he went on and on towards the city, which each time showed itself nearer and more beautiful to his eyes. But each time he felt less anxiety to arrive.

Still he had not finished with the difficulties. The path soon shortened, forming a terrible ravine; only to think of crossing it was more than he could dream of. Rupert believed his hopes broken, and sat down disheartened on a stone.

At that moment a vulture of great size came down from the top of a mountain and, drawing near him, said:

"Do you wish to go across? Well, give me a piece of your heart."

"Take it, and carry me over," said Rupert, desperate.

The vulture thrust its beak into Rupert's chest and took out a good piece of heart. At once it seized our lad with its claws and carried him to the other side of the abyss.

Now he was at the very gates of Fortune. He could already count the number of towers which raised themselves above the high walls, and took his happiness for granted—if that consists in money. At the gate they stopped him. There heart was contraband, and therefore they took out what remained of it and put a pretty one inside of him, made of steel, but hard as a diamond. Only one little fibre escaped their search, which passed unnoticed behind the metal heart.

"At last I am inside," said Rupert to himself; but, strangely enough, the city of gold produced neither surprise nor joy.

"What do I want riches for?" he exclaimed, "if I have lost my heart and with it my illusions?" And he walked through the city, looking with great disdain at those riches which were within reach of his hand and which so much tempted his ambition before.

That dazzling brilliance began to disturb him.

"Here it seems," he said to himself, "there is nothing else but gold. Cursed metal, which has cost me my heart. Goodness me! Who will give me back my little heart?"

He looked for friends, but did not succeed in finding them, because those people had hearts of steel, and Rupert felt that that little fibre that remained of his own made him suffer atrociously.

Without friends or affection, in that city of gold, Rupert remembered his parents and his brother and bitterly lamented his fate.

And then he resolved to return to the little white house of his own village and to live in it as God had ordered. On going out of the city he felt a strange joy. But that accursed steel heart made him suffer horribly, only the little fibre which remained of his own beat for joy in his breast. He took the first path he found, and then encountered no difficulties. It seemed that wings had grown on his feet. He went down hill, and so walked very quickly. When he arrived at his village he was as poor as before, and moreover that cold, hard heart did not let him breathe. It beat with the regularity of a clock, tic-tac, tic-tac!

His brother was the first to come out and meet him, full of joy. He embraced him, kissed him, and accompanied him home, transported with gladness.

But the steel heart did not allow Rupert to rejoice. Tears did nor run to his eyes, and his chest felt as if a hand was pressing on it.

His old father strained him to his bosom, but not even he

succeeded in moving that hard heart. Rupert felt an extraordinary anguish.

But his mother arrived running, out of breath, towards her son, and embraced him weeping, and her tears fell on Rupert's heart. Then, oh, the power of a mother's love! That steel heart quickened its beats and, unable to resist any longer, jumped out, just as a broken spring of a watch jumps out. The little fibre was already a new heart and Rupert a happy man.

And when they spoke to him of riches he said:

"God will give them if he deem it right, but don't seek them by short cuts at the expense of your heart and illusions."

THE GARDEN OF HEALTH

A boy of twelve years, named Enrique, was taking a walk one day in the outskirts of his village. He was very sad because his little sister was ill and the doctors said she would soon die.

"Poor Luisa!" exclaimed the boy sobbing. "So pretty and to have to leave this world so soon!"

Enrique sat down on some stones to weep over his sorrow, and there prayed to heaven for his sister's life. A kid who was grazing near the spot heard the sound of his lamentations and drawing near the disconsolate boy said:

"Calm yourself and I will try and save Luisa."

"How?" asked Enrique, startled at hearing the kid speak.

"You have the remedy within reach of your hand. Look there, to the right in that spring, and you will see a ring which was left there and forgotten by the magician Agrajes. Put it on and ask to go to the Garden of Health, and immediately it will take you there. Ask there for the Blue Ivy whose juice will cure your sister, and if they deny it to you, use the ring and you will see."

"Ay, little kid, anything to please you. Will you tell me who you are?"

"Well, you can see: a kid with its horns and all."

"But kids don't speak, and you do."

"That is because I am a well-bred and compassionate kid. Anyway, I cannot tell you who I am. If you are grateful you will know. Meanwhile, don't lose time, and do what I tell you."

Enrique saw, indeed, a gold ring which was on the edge of the spring: he seized it and on it saw certain mysterious signs engraved.

He put it on the ring finger of his left hand and said in a loud voice: "To the Garden of Health."

Scarcely had he finished saying these words than a cloud descended and carried him through the air at lightning speed.

In a few minutes he found himself at the gates of a beautiful garden surrounded by a silver fence with golden ornaments. At the gate there were two maidens, one in white and the other in black. The one in white had a fresh and smiling face; the other was sad and taciturn. The former carried an apple in her hand, the latter bore a scythe.

"Who are you?" asked Enrique.

"I am Life," said the first.

"I, Death," replied the second in dismal tones.

"What have you come here for?" they asked the boy.

"I have come for a branch of Blue Ivy to cure my sister with."

"I cannot give it to you without the permission of this maiden," said Life, motioning towards Death.

"I will not permit it, because Luisa belongs to me. She is a prize which I will not give up," growled Death angrily.

Life smiled sadly and turning to Enrique said:

"I cannot give you what you wish, but bear in mind that you can take it without my giving it to you."

"Well, then, I will enter, cost what it may," exclaimed the boy.

"You shall not enter alive," shouted Death, brandishing her scythe.

"Oh, yes, he will, if he is quick," said Life provoked. "Do not meddle with this boy who is mine for many years."

"We shall see now."

Enrique jumped over the threshold of the garden gate

and Death dealt him a terrible blow with her scythe, which would have deprived him of existence if at that moment Life had not made him smell the apple which she held in her hand and which quite cured him.

So Enrique passed between Life and Death into the Garden of Health and once inside commenced his quest in order to see if he could find the famous ivy which was to cure his little sister. It was difficult to find it among so many and such different plants as filled that beautiful garden where was medicine for every illness; but Enrique was resolved to find it, and passed through, one after another, the avenues of trees which crossed the park of health in all directions.

"I am the Red Celery, that cures all chest diseases," said a highly colored celery plant bowing to Enrique.

"And I am the Spanish Onion, that cures the kidneys."

"And I am the Valerian, that cures the nerves."

"And I this, and I the other," cried the other plants and trees.

"That's enough!" shouted Enrique, "otherwise you will drive me mad."

"I cure madness," cried a shrub from the bottom of the garden.

"What I want is the Blue Ivy," exclaimed the boy.

"Here I am," cried the plant alluded to, "but I am kept closely guarded."

Enrique searched everywhere, without ascertaining where the precious plant was, but he always seemed to hear the noise in different places.

The trees laughed at Enrique's despair.

"And who keeps you so hidden?" said Enrique, stopping still for a moment.

"Death hides me in order that you may not find me. You have passed near and have not seen me. Your sister will die if you cannot find me."

Enrique now did not know what to do, until he presently remembered his ring.

"Ring of Agrajes, I want to see the Blue Ivy," he exclaimed.

Instantly he saw, within reach of his hand, a lovely ivy that, clinging to an oak, displayed beautiful leaves to the winds.

"Do not cut me now," cried the Ivy, "because your sister is going to die, and you will not arrive in time. Death is now close to her bedside."

"Ring of Agrajes," exclaimed Enrique at once, "bring Death to me tied up."

Hardly had he finished saying it than Death appeared quite dishevelled, without her scythe, her elbows tied together like a criminal. All the health-giving plants began to applaud.

"Bravo, bravo!" they cried.

"Don't spare her; she is our enemy!" shouted some.

"Don't let her go, and the world will be grateful to you!" said others.

"What have you done to my sister?" said Enrique, angrily.

"Nothing yet, but as soon as you let me go you will see," answered Death.

"Well, if you wait until you are free before killing her, my little sister will die of old age. Ring, give this shameful woman a thrashing."

Immediately a number of sticks came through the air and commenced to bestow a fine thrashing upon Death.

The latter screamed like a mouse whose tail has been trodden on, and heaped insults on the boy, threatening to kill him as soon as she was free.

"Do not spare her!" said Enrique at each insult.

And the blows again descended on Death like rain. One knocked an eye out, another knocked all her teeth out, although it must be admitted they were false, and another took her hair out by the roots, leaving her head quite bald.

Then Enrique cut a sprig of the Ivy and said to the ring, "Take me to my sister's side."

Immediately he found himself at the bedside, where all the family were weeping over the approaching death of the girl.

"Here is something which will cure my little sister," said the boy.

And drawing near her, he squeezed into her mouth the juice of the fresh ivy he had plucked in the Garden of Health.

The girl at once opened her eyes and called her mother, and, amidst the general surprise, asked to be dressed.

The family would not do so until the doctor said that indeed she was well and sound. They all complimented Enrique enthusiastically, until at length the boy said:

"All this is due to a kid, and I must go and thank her."

He went to the same place where he had met the kid, but did not see her. In vain he ran around in all directions. But he had not got the ring of Agrajes for nothing.

"Ring," he said, "bring me the kid that was here a short time ago."

And the kid appeared.

"What do you want of me, Enrique?" asked the animal.

"To thank you, and to ask how I may serve you," answered Enrique.

"I see that you are grateful, and I wish you to know who I am. I am called Atala, and am the daughter of Agrajes, the magician. I put my father's ring beside you with the object that you might be able to save your sister."

"I should like to know you in your real form and not in that of a kid."

"Well, here I am," exclaimed Atala.

And thereupon she transformed herself into a lovely girl of more or less Enrique's age.

"How pretty you are!" exclaimed the boy. "Come home and play with my little sister, who is now quite well, thanks to you."

"I can deny you nothing while you wear this ring," answered the girl.

"No, take it, I beg of you."

Atala disappeared at once, and when Enrique thought she had gone never to return, she reappeared smiling, and said:

"I have been for a moment to ask my father's permission to accompany you."

They went to Enrique's house together, and he introduced her to his parents as Luisa's savior. They fêted her with cakes and sweets, and on saying good-bye she promised to come back every afternoon to play with her little friends.

One day Agrajes himself visited Enrique's home, to make the acquaintance of the family of which his daughter spoke so much, and on going away he touched in a special way an old chest.

"Open it, presently," he said on saying farewell.

On opening it they found it full to the brim of gold coins.

On it there was a paper which said: "A present from Agrajes to two very nice children."

With that money Enrique followed his career and Luisa had a splendid dowry, and with that and the love of their parents and friends they were two very happy beings.

KHING-CHU-FU

Khing-Chu-Fu, Empress of China, was doing her hair when her maids who, on their knees witnessed the delicate operation of artistically arranging the imperial hair of her majesty, burst into cries of admiration scarcely repressed by the etiquette of the palace.

"What is the matter?" Khing-Chu-Fu deigned to ask, turning her head.

"Ah, lady!" exclaimed the maids in a chorus. "Brahma has deigned to favor you with a sign of his protection."

"And what is that?" inquired the empress.

"A silver thread that appears in your beautiful hair."

"That is to say I have a white hair."

"So it is called among simple mortals, but in the Daughter of the Sun they are threads of silver, to which poets spontaneously sing verses under the penalty of being quartered like dogs."

"Let the seers and astrologers come at this very moment. I must know what this foretells."

Five minutes afterwards the royal boudoir was full of moustached men with eye-protectors, who, kneeling, waited to be consulted.

"Today a white hair has appeared in my head!" exclaimed the empress.

The seers tugged at their moustaches in desperation, leaving the floor covered with hairs.

"Hail!" said the eldest, "Daughter of the Sun, who hast all the brilliance of the diamond, the beauty of the iris, the wisdom of Confucius, and the sweetness of the honey! This silver thread foretells a terrible calamity in the empire. Know that Brahma has decreed—it horrifies me to say so!—that one of your imperial teeth will commence to ache."

Terror was depicted on every countenance, and all who witnessed this scene pulled their pigtails, a sign of terrible desperation among the Chinese. The pages and maids groaned in chorus; the mandarins sat down on their hats, passing the time by eating tangerine oranges and rubbing their eyes with the peel. The news spread into the city, and very soon the whole of Peking[3] came out into the streets and places weeping salt tears over the terrible aching of the *too—*, for simple subjects were forbidden to pronounce completely the names of the imperial members or other parts of their illustrious sovereign's body.

"The too—, the too—!" shouted the maddened people, making Peking seem like an immense enclosure of bulls: and as if to make the illusion still more complete, there were not lacking people who produced cattle-bells with which the faithful are called to the pagoda—the church of the Chinese.

In those days there came to Peking a young Spaniard, a native of Seville[4], a sharp and witty youth, who had arrived at the capital of the Chinese Empire after having wandered over half the world on foot, without money and without shame. He was thought to be very wide-awake and even clever, and all because he had been a groom and bull-ring attendant in his own town where he was nicknamed Pinchauvas.

Well, our Pinchauvas was astonished to see the desperation of those Chinese and above all when he heard the sound of too—! too—! which made him fear he was going to meet a drove of bulls. In case it was so, he thought it better to climb

3 Peking refers to the Chinese city of Beijing.
4 Seville is the capital of the autonomous region of Andaulsia in Southern Spain.

up to the first window which came to hand.

He had hardly reached the window, when from the interior of the house came forth a hand, and then an arm, which, catching hold of him firmly by the neck, pulled him up and made him enter the house in a most original way.

The arm was that of a palace guard who, on seeing our Sevillian climbing up to a window of one of the imperial rooms, detained him in order to deliver him up to justice.

This crime was a terrible one. In China it was something daring to profane one of the windows of the empress! That crime was punishable, at the least, with death.

The worst of it was that Pinchauvas did not know a word of Chinese, and was therefore amazed when the guard said to him, with a terrible air:

"Kun-chin-pon-ton!"

"What is this fellow saying to me?" thought Pinchauvas. "He seems to have a stomach-ache and is telling me that he has indigestion. Well, let him get better." And he shrugged his shoulders.

But the guard was nasty and, seizing him again by the neck, took him through the passages of the palace to the rooms of the great chancellor. The latter was found praying to God that the terrible prediction might not be fulfilled, as it might cost him his destiny. "If the empress's tooth hurts her, she will hurt me," said he.

So when he was told of the horrible sacrilege committed by a foreigner, he became exceedingly angry and wished to have him beheaded.

"Take me to this youth, that I may settle him," he said to the guard.

And facing the Spaniard he said sharply:

"Kun-chin-pon-ton?"

"Another stomach-ache? The same as the horses in the bull-ring. But perhaps they have worries!"

By good fortune the great chancellor spoke broken French and Pinchauvas also, so that at last they almost came to understand each other.

"And what did you do in your country?" asked the chancellor.

"I? A wise monkey[5]."

The chancellor did not understand the word monkey, but did understand the word wise, and full of joy he said:

"I am going to ask you a question, and if you answer me rightly, count on my protection."

The chancellor then informed Pinchauvas of the cause that had sown such sorrow in Peking, and the lad, smiling, said to him with the greatest composure:

"Is that all? Well I will restore calm to the Chinese Empire. I will make this white hair disappear and with it the presages of these charlatans. What has the hair to do with the teeth? Introduce me to the empress and you will see something interesting."

"I will, but it would not be well for the empress to see you in these clothes. May God make your days happy! We must make you look decent!"

And taking him to the bathroom, he placed him in the hands of his slaves who, in a twinkling, perfumed and clothed him in beautiful robes of silk and gold.

Pinchauvas, accompanied by the great chancellor, went to the imperial rooms, and there, on account of the person who accompanied him being the head of the government,

5   A wise monkey is a boy attendant in a Spanish bull-ring.

had only to wait in eleven ante-chambers, after which he was shown into the imperial presence.

"Here I bring you, celebrated princess, the most famous and wise necromancer of the world," said the chancellor, who must have been fond of exaggerating. "A whirlwind made him fall on this palace dragging him from far lands, and in the centre of the whirlwind it seems to me I saw great Confucius, who held him by the neck."

"Rise, wise man!" said the empress sweetly.

Pinchauvas did not move.

"Get up, wise man!" repeated the chancellor in French.

"Do you mean me?" exclaimed Pinchauvas. And with one bound he stood up.

"Bow down, or you are a dead man," shouted the chancellor to him.

"I don't want to," answered the youth.

"What does he say?" inquired the princess.

"That he must see the silver thread that Brahma presented you with this morning."

"Look at it!" said the queen with emphasis.

And taking out the seven hundred hair-pins and the three hundred packing needles with which she adorned herself, she let her silky black hair fall down, and amongst it could be seen one hair as white as snow.

Pinchauvas advanced, with more fear than shame and his mind made up, seized the hair, and, making signs as if in prayer, sharply pulled it out. The queen gave a scream and Pinchauvas, approaching a window, threw out the white hair, the cause of the misfortune of the Chinese Empire.

"Ah!" exclaimed the queen, "do you return Brahma his gift? What a marvellous man! He deserves a thousand rewards. For the present you will cede to him your post, and from today he will be my chancellor; and, so that you will not be troubled, I will hang you this afternoon with a rope that I made for you some days ago."

"What an honor for the family, lady!" said the chancellor, terrified. "Do you wish me to translate your proposal to the wise man?"

"Do so at once."

The poor man translated with complete fidelity what the queen had said, and then Pinchauvas told the chancellor that he would only accept his post on condition that he was given him as his secretary.

The empress acceded to Pinchauvas' request, and granted him the royal seal as a sign of his unlimited authority.

"So that I can do what I like?" he asked.

"Whatever your highness wishes! Now, I am going to present you to the high functionaries of the palace."

He received them all with gestures of amiable protection, and the chancellor translated what he said.

"See here," said Pinchauvas, "let them bring me that Chinaman who seized me by the neck two hours ago."

"Seized your highness by your venerable neck?" indignantly asked the secretary.

"Does your highness wish us to burn him alive or simply to hang him?"

"I want you to bring him here safe and sound."

"Really, does your highness wish to strangle him with your own hands? He does not deserve such an extraordinary honor."

They brought the poor guard into the presence of Pinchauvas, and when they told him he was the new chancellor he almost died of terror.

"And now shall I really give you stomach-ache?" asked Pinchauvas, deliberately, raising his hand to his neck, which still hurt him.

The guard thought these were signs to hang him, and they would have done so, but for the opportune intervention of the brand new chancellor, who, besides pardoning the unfortunate man, conferred a high post upon him close to his person.

Pinchauvas has now learned Chinese and is called Pinchu-chu, which means the wisest of the wise. And when he remembers his youth, he says inwardly:

"What would those poor horses in the bull-ring of Seville have said if they had been told that they had had the honor of being guided by the future Chancellor of China!"

> *THE FUTURE*
> *IS A SEALED BOOK*
> *OF WHICH*
> *GOD ALONE*
> *HAS THE KEY*

CARABI! CARABO!

Little Arthur once went out in his garden, and on sitting down at the foot of an acacia he heard a cloverleaf saying:

"I am Antonio."

And one of the points of the leaf changed into the head of a small boy.

"I am Juanita!" exclaimed the second point of the leaf. And a tiny girl appeared.

"And I Perico."

And another head showed itself beside the others.

"Good gracious!" exclaimed little Arthur, "this could be set to music like the rats' dance." He approached the clover but now saw nothing: nor was he quite sure which was the marvellous leaf where he had seen those three children as small as they were beautiful.

"Well, I shan't rest until I have seen into this," said the boy.

So the following day, at the same time, he re-seated himself in the same place, and presently a sigh: the cloverleaf began to tremble and immediately the little heads appeared in succession, saying, as on the previous day;

"I am Antonio."

"I am Juanita."

"And I Perico."

"And I Arthur!" exclaimed the boy, showing himself suddenly, and seizing the mysterious leaf, "Either you tell me who you are or I will pull you up by the roots."

The stem trembled, and from another near by came forth a very sad voice saying: "Don't kill them for heaven's sake, they are quite innocent of doing any wrong: come back to-night at twelve o'clock and you will be amazed at what you see."

Contented, the boy obeyed, and went away resolved to come back again that night. And so about half-past eleven Arthur went out into the garden, and hiding himself amongst a group of magnolias, waited until the stated hour struck. Scarcely had the church clock chimed the last stroke of midnight than a noise was heard in the air, and there appeared on the ground a horse as white as snow and provided with wings which it shook at the moment of touching the earth. From the wings there came millions of drops of water which fell in a fine rain on the plants in the garden. The effect was magical; instantly all the plants took on the most unexpected forms. The cloverleaf was changed into a grand stand covered with a splendid canopy of velvet and gold, and on three gilded arm-chairs sat three children of dazzling beauty wearing rich clothing, in which elegance and sumptuousness struggled for supremacy.

The acacias were transformed into towers of shining silver full of soldiers, who presented arms to the children in token of homage. The group of magnolias was a stone castle, with a steel drawbridge hanging by chains of red silk interwoven with gold. A crowd of pages in bright uniforms, soldiers on horseback provided with lances and with glittering helmets adorned with airy plumes, walked about the garden in all directions. Life animated all those beings passing before the astonished eyes of little Arthur, who, hidden behind a tower, could see what happened without being seen himself. Such was his amazement that, thinking he was dreaming, he hit himself in the most fleshy part of the body, and noticing that it hurt, convinced himself that he was not dreaming. Thereupon the horse neighed, and they all stopped still, full of terror.

"Carabi! Carabo! Two minutes are left you of becoming like me," shouted the horse.

On hearing him they all wept, except the three princes who rose, exclaiming:

"Treacherous magician, God wills that you pay for your crimes."

The horse rose on two legs and after a terrific neigh shouted: "Carabi! Carabo!" and immediately they all resumed their original forms. The horse gave a jump in order to rise in the air and commenced his flight, but this time he was not alone; for when waving his tail it caught up good little Arthur, winding itself round his body. The boy clung to it in order not to fall, and when he tried to find out where he was, he discovered himself in the air more than a thousand yards from the ground. Then he yelled with all the strength that fear gives, without paying any attention to the neighing of the horse which, turning its head, said to him: "Leave go, or I will dash your brains out with a kick."

But little Arthur remembered that if he let go he would certainly be killed, while it was by no means sure that the horse could reach him with his feet, because he had climbed up to the top part of the tail, where he hung on with one hand, while with the other he caught hold of the other end, so that he sat on the doubled-up tail as on a trapeze.

The horse landed out half a dozen kicks, which only hurt the clouds; he turned his head in order to see where to bite that customer who had got the better of him; but his wings hindered him, and the only other vengeance he could take was to snort. This he did, making such a noise that it could have been heard for miles around.

"What a storm!" exclaimed little Arthur.

"That is the wind I swallow in my flight," said the horse.

"That is not wind, it must be a hurricane let loose."

Then the horse began to descend towards the earth, passing through clouds and breaking up fogs, until, at dawn, he arrived at a lovely palace whose roof of gold and precious stones opened of its own accord to let that singular horse pass through. He alighted on the floor of an enormous room in the palace, and when on firm ground said:

"Will you please leave go of me."

"That depends," said little Arthur, "because I am just beginning to like this way of travelling."

"Well, my son, I am sorry, but your goose is cooked for ever."

So saying he began to butt round the room with the object of smashing poor little Arthur to pieces; but the latter, firm as firm could be, would not leave go even if he were killed. Then the horse sat down to see if he could crush the boy with his weight, but the latter, by a clever movement, dropped clear of the crupper and sat down on the floor.

"Here!" he exclaimed, "don't do any more such silly things; if you want to throw me off, you will have to tear your tail off first."

"Not if I know it," shouted the magician, "rather let us make an agreement. What do you want in order to let me go?"

"First, you must tell me the story of the enchanted children in my garden."

"I will not."

"Well, now I shall pull out a hair of your tail by way of punishment," and dragging out one of them he made the horse neigh with pain.

"So, I shall pull them out one by one until you are as hairless as a hired horse."

"No, you have persuaded me. Listen to the story you ask me for. You must know that these youngsters are the children of the great King of Samarcanda, Ali-Tebelin, who is a great enemy of mine. I was then condemned to be ridden by any cavalier who wished to do so, thanks to the enchantment of a relative on my mother's side, who knew how to do these things better than I. Not finding any better way of passing the three years as saddle-horse which had been imposed upon me, I entered the stables of Ali-Tebelin, who several times had me thrashed on the frivolous pretext that I bit whoever wanted to ride on me, kicked anybody who came near, and one day gave the king himself a terrible bite. Angry on account of this injustice I promised myself to have my revenge, and when the period of my enchantment was finished, I became, in my turn, an enchanter, and taking a bottle of water gathered by me from the clouds, I caused the king's court to be transformed into a garden which I transported to your house. Every night I go to it, and as my wings are wet with the water from the clouds, which is the thing that has the property of changing them into their original shapes, I shake my wings, and after enjoying myself for a while I enchant them again with my word. Now you know all, will you leave me in peace?"

"Now less than ever," said the boy: "because if I let you go, you will be revenged on me as on them, so that I shan't leave you until you take me back to my home. At this very moment you will give me something to eat. Go somewhere slowly where there is something to put inside one; if you don't I will skin you."

The horse stamped on the floor, and at once several tables covered with eatables appeared. With one hand, while with the other he held on, Arthur ate of what seemed best to him, and when he was satisfied, said: "At this very instant you will take me home." The horse, resigned, took to flight again, rose up in the air, and flew towards Arthur's garden. Passing through the clouds, Arthur got all his clothing wet, being drenched with that precious liquid. When they arrived, and before the horse had time to turn round, little Arthur ran away and took refuge in his home. His precaution was very wise, because the magician followed him with the object of biting him, but when he was ready to do so the boy was already in the house. The horse had only stretched his wings and disappeared on the horizon when Arthur went into the garden again, and shaking his clothes, let the cloud-water with which he was soaked fall upon the plants. At once all the enchanted beings recovered their original shape, and saw with surprise that it was not the magician who disenchanted them. On seeing such surprise, little Arthur advanced towards the grand stand and said to the princes:

"Children of Ali-Tebelin, I have the pleasure of informing you that you are free; but vanish from here quickly, because at twelve o'clock to-night the magician will return."

"Thanks, kind boy," said one of the princes, "but we will not go away from here without giving the magician a surprise and bestowing on him something that will make him stare."

So they fastened some strong ropes to the towers, and that night, when the horse arrived, before he knew what had happened, he found himself tied by the neck, wings, and feet, and all the warriors and pages, provided with strong cords, rained such a shower of blows on him that he did not know where he was.

"Take that, Carabi!"

"Take that, Carabo!" they shouted. And the hail of lashes was such that the magician begged them for pardon.

"No pardon!" shouted little Arthur, "you can stay there till your feet drop off."

Such were his groans that at last little Arthur, full of compassion, went up to him and said:

"How can we set you free when we should only be exposing ourselves to your vengeance?"

"To avoid that the only thing you have to do is to pull out the longest feather in each wing, and then I shall be deprived of power."

This Arthur did, and immediately the magician took human shape, it being seen that he was a horrid dwarf who could hardly move. They touched him again with the feathers and he was changed into a caged parrot which began to shout, "Carabi! Carabo! It's all over with me now!"

Arthur informed his parents, telling them all about his extraordinary adventure, and begged them for permission to accompany the princes. Little Arthur's parents were astonished to see their garden changed into a fortress; and on becoming acquainted with the series of events which, without their knowledge, had occurred, granted their permission and at once the expedition was organised. Little Arthur mounted one of the magic feathers, bearing the princess behind him. The princes bestrode the other feather, and all the rest clung to each other. At a given signal they all flew away, and in a twinkling found themselves in their own country.

There little Arthur was splendidly presented with a pair of socks and several boxes of toys, his efforts being rewarded by a long and happy life in the bosom of his family.

THE AUTHOR OF THE WALL

Ninin was reading in a newspaper: "They are beginning to pull down the great wall of China."

"Is that so? What! Does the newspaper say so?"

"Look at it yourself," says Ninin showing me the paper where the news was printed.

"Well," I answered, "I am glad, because of what use ... Would you like me to tell you a story?"

"Is it about the Chinese wall?"

"You will see. Once there was a king in the country called Tsi-Ching-Hoang-Ti (what a name!) with a very long pigtail. The Chinese are recognised by their pigtails, while, in Spain, we only know toreadors[6] for the same reason.

"Well, the king in my story had few teeth, but a very long pigtail, and had a stomach which could have held half his kingdom. What a wolfish appetite! Every five minutes he yawned, and in every room of the palace there were attendants whose only mission was to place a boiled egg in the monarch's mouth as soon as he commenced to open it. And what a mouth! Once some one absent-mindedly placed his memorial in it thinking he was putting it in the letter box. One night, while he was sleeping, Tsi-Ching-Hoang-Ti (Dear me! what work to call a person thus!) gave a tremendous kick and, sitting up in bed, shouted:

"'I have an idea!'

"The guards, electrified, shouted:

"'The emperor has an idea!'

"And all the functionaries of the palace and the imperial family came to the regal room to congratulate their emperor.

---

6   Toreadors are bullfighters.

"'What a happy day!' they exclaimed. 'It is the first time that such a thing has happened in China. To have an idea.'

"'Yes, dear subjects,' said the monarch tenderly, 'I have an idea to prevent the disasters caused by the Ta⁷tars who fall upon us every Monday and Tuesday. And this idea is...' (they all knelt down to hear the sublime words)'... to ask you if anything has occurred to you to avoid them.'

"'Well thought out!' said the courtiers in a chorus.

"'Therefore I will begin by asking the minister of war.'

"The minister touched the floor with his head and says:

"'Sire, between now and tomorrow I will answer your majesty: but I have heard briefly that, in order to avoid being overrun, what we ought to do is not to let them into the country.'

"'Eureka!' exclaimed the emperor. 'This being the idea of a minister of war is not at all bad. Let the audience rise; goodbye till tomorrow.'

"And chewing a boiled egg which they had just put into his mouth he lay down in bed again and went to sleep, after having formed that tremendous idea which had been forty years in coming.

"That very night the minister of war consulted the captain-generals, these their lieutenant-generals, these the camp-marshals, and so on until they came to the sergeants, and these asked the soldiers, without finding any who dared to propose a plan, until a soldier of the awkward squad, and the most awkward of the squad, said, 'Well, close the way with a mud-wall.'

"'Enough, stupid!' shouted the officer, and gave him a

7 The Tatars were Turkish-speaking people who originated in Central Asia, and refers to the clan of people who performed the Turco-Mongol invasions on the Near East and Europe.

punch.

"The officer gave the idea as his own to the major, and the latter passed it on to the lieutenant. The major also appropriated the idea and they made him a colonel, and so all were advanced except the poor soldier, who rubbed his face with sand to take away the mark of the blow.

"When the minister of war explained how convenient it would be to build a wall the emperor was charmed, the court was charmed, and everybody was charmed.

"'And they said that my army was a flock of geese!' exclaimed the king.

"Following up the plan, the dimensions of the wall and the materials it was to be made of were discussed. One engineer said that it had to be six hundred leagues in length, and that to collect materials for it, it was necessary to ask the genie of stones for them, this being the only one who could help them in such an extraordinary enterprise.

"Moreover, the difficulty was that the emperor himself had to go and ask this aid: and who would disturb his majesty with such a long journey!

"'That does not matter!' exclaimed Tsi-Ching-Hoang-Ti, 'provided there are boiled eggs on the way.'

"The emperor and the engineer entered a palanquin and shortly afterwards set out to look for the genie of the stones. Behind followed another palanquin with a kitchen and then a hundred more palanquins full of boiled eggs. After twenty days' march the expedition arrived at the foot of the mountains of Chuang and rested there. Only the emperor and the engineer could go up to the abode of the genie, situated between horrible precipices, and therefore his majesty and his companion filled their pockets with boiled eggs for the journey. When they arrived at the foot of the grotto where the genie dwelt, a rain of rubbish met them which nearly swept them away. A bump appeared on the emperor which looked as if one of the hundred thousand eggs he had eaten had come out there; a wicked tile had torn out the architect's plait by the roots which caused the poor man much pain, because his pigtail was already three yards long and was still growing. The king became angry and went on valorously disposed to behead the daring rascal who had stoned him, and at last they found themselves in the chamber of the genie Marmolillo. The latter received them with great courtesy, asking them the object of their visit. When the emperor told him, the genie gave his forehead a slap, which sounded like stones knocking together.

"'Well, it is true!' he exclaimed. 'And it had not occurred to me! The truth is that I have a head of stone. Well, all right,' he added, 'I will help you, and with my aid and that of all the Chinese it may be that within twenty days you will see it finished.'

"And so, when Tsi-Ching-Hoang-Ti returned to the court, he arranged that all Chinamen from fifteen to fifty years should go to the frontier to begin the work: and in a few days sixty million workmen were working on the wall and setting themselves to work with truly Chinese ardor.

"That was twenty-one centuries ago, Mr. Ninin, so that you had not yet studied the map when the wall was already finished, which, as was seen afterwards, was of no use only to make the Tatars carry ladders. They came back and invaded China and made themselves kings of it. The present dynasty is Tatar, the same as the celebrated sauce which you like so much."

"Good, but I should like the story to have some sort of a

moral."

"Well, here is one: that the real walls to defend ourselves from our enemies are our faith in God and in the justice of our cause."

THE DEVIL'S TOURNAMENT

Great anger filled the breast of the very ugly Don Teobaldo de Miguelturra as he rode his horse at full gallop after a cunning hare. Lance at rest he pursued it, blind with fury, for the wicked animal from time to time stopped, sat down on its hind paws, and made amusing grimaces at its pursuer.

The latter, filled with wrath, did not leave off using his spurs, and followed after the animal, loudly calling it a coward, rogue, and thief.

"Wait, wait!" he shouted; "you will have to pay for all this! What a fine stew I shall make with you this evening!"

And he rode on like a madman, leaping streams, rocks, and pits. But it seemed as if wings had grown on the hare's feet, such were its leaps, while fleeing from the proposed stew. And at each instant it turned round and jocularly made signs with its ears and fore-paws, and smiled in that amusing way which disturbed the knight so much.

"Even if you hide yourself in the very middle of the earth, I shall reach you," he roared.

And he again spurred on his horse, which was nearly frantic, excited by pain and the shouting of its rider.

A moment arrived in which the knight almost had it within lance thrust, but once more it commenced to gain ground.

"One effort more, my horse," shouted Don Teobaldo, but in vain. In going up a very steep slope the poor animal fell dead from fatigue, and the rider also was quite dazed.

As soon as he could he disengaged himself from the stirrups, and throwing down his useless lance beside the dead horse, Don Teobaldo unsheathed his sword, victorious in a hundred fights, in order to pursue to the very end that hare which had stopped very tranquilly on a rock from which it made fun of the knight at its ease.

This raised the hunter's indignation to its highest, and in a moment of anger he exclaimed:

"I would give a year of my life to run my sword through you."

The hare, on hearing this, gave a jump and fell at Don Teobaldo's feet, who cut it into two pieces. The spitted hare said to him before dying: "It will cost you a year of your life; don't forget it."

The man shuddered and would have liked to undo the mischief, but now it was too late.

"And to think that such a little beast should make me lose three hundred and sixty-five days of my life!" he cried. And, full of rage, he trampled on the hare until he was quite tired.

But on raising his eyes once more he saw another exactly the same as that he had killed, and which made the same gestures as the first.

Then he could not any longer contain himself, and started to run after the second hare, entangling his spurs in the under-growth and stumbling and falling at every step.

Like one who took no interest the hare went slowly to its lair, and after it our enraged Don Teobaldo, resolved to make a terrible hash of the jesting animal.

"This seems to be a thing of the devil," he said. "All the hares have agreed to make fun of me."

At length, after a good while, Don Teobaldo, with his tongue hanging out, arrived at a kind of cave, in the black depths of which he lost sight of the hare.

"Well, now, I have to find you even if you are the devil

himself in person."

"Your servant," said a voice of rare quality; and a man with a strange face and eyes of fire presented himself before Don Teobaldo, saluting him with burlesque courtesy.

"Caramba!" exclaimed Don Teobaldo, without being frightened, because he was a very valorous man. "If I must tell the truth, I wished to know you personally."

"And do you not feel afraid?"

"Not at all. And since you are so familiar with me, I shall treat you in the same way. I want to make an arrangement with you."

"Speak."

"First answer me: are you the hare that I pursued?"

"The same. I knew that you were engaged in an affair and wished to speak to me, and brought you to my house so that we could talk comfortably."

And the devil started laughing, flames shooting out of his mouth. It was a sign that he was happy.

"Well, you shall see. You must know that tomorrow the tournament in which the hand of the king's daughter is to be disputed will take place. The victor will become hereditary prince, and I, frankly, wish to occupy the post. It is therefore necessary that you make me conquer in the fray."

"And what will you give me in exchange?"

"Whatever you ask me."

"That you make the princess forget her faith in God. I already have you, and I want the princess."

"Agreed."

"Agreed."

And the devil and Don Teobaldo shook hands. The latter drew his back, saying:

"How you burn."

The devil said to him:

"Tomorrow, at the hour of the fight, a squire in black armor will come and see you. I will give you a cuirass made in such a way that it cannot be pierced through; a shield which will dazzle and stupefy your adversaries if only looked at; a charmed sword, a touch with which will produce death; and a horse as black as ebony which has the advantage of requiring neither curb nor spurs: you will only wear them as ornaments.... In a word, the horse—will be me."

"Oh, thanks, but I am sorry to trouble you."

"Don't let us say a word about this affair. I have resolved to carry away the soul of this princess, who wearies me with her prayers and psalms, and I have not been able to make her sin, even in thought."

And the devil caught up Don Teobaldo with his cape and left him at the door of his house, after passing through the air at a prodigious speed. On disappearing, he said in his ear: "Good-bye till tomorrow."

On the following day the city was decorated with pennons and banners. The entire population flocked to the place where the hand of the beautiful princess, whose virtues everybody praised highly, was to be won in open contest.

Thirty knights took part in the struggle, and as they were the bravest in the kingdom the spectacle promised to be interesting, though barbarous; but such were the customs of those times.

The king and the court occupied the grand stand, the princess being in the front row. The public took the rest of the seats, and the heralds announced that the jousts were about to commence.

Don Teobaldo appeared in the foreground upon a beautiful black horse, large black plumes waved over the crest of his helmet, and the armor which he wore was also black.

On seeing his proud countenance one could not doubt his certainty of obtaining the victory.

The signal was given, and another valiant knight came into the arena and rushed upon horrible Don Teobaldo at his horse's full gallop.

When he was near, the devil's friend oscillated his shield, and his adversary, without being able to prevail, fell to the ground unconscious.

Another and another and another, and twenty more, went forth to fight and suffered the same fate. Whoever resisted the mysterious action of the shield, fell dead from a blow of the sword, even when only touched with the flat of it.

The people gave shouts of despair on account of the horror which that man inspired in them. The princess was on the point of losing consciousness from terror on seeing that terrible spouse who was offering her his disgrace.

"Heaven!" she exclaimed, "death before being the wife of that wicked man."

And now, the last champion having suffered the same defeat as the others, they were about to proclaim Don Teobaldo conqueror, and therefore the husband of the princess, when the trumpet sounded, announcing that a noble knight asked permission to take part in the struggle.

The king looked at his daughter and, on seeing her so sorrow-stricken, gave the desired permission, with the remote hope that the newcomer, whoever he might be, would vanquish the terrible champion.

They requested him to tell his name and surname, but

the knight said:

"My name is Miguel; my surname I reserve until after the fight, if I emerge victorious, but rest assured that there is no one more noble on earth."

And he rode into the lists, arousing a murmur of admiration; his armor was all white as ermine[7], and the plumes of his helmet were also white.

White, of a dazzling white, was the beautiful horse he rode.

Don Teobaldo was greatly impressed by the sight, and more so the devil, who with a neigh said: "I am glad you have come to fight, Miguel; we have an old account to settle."

And turning his head to Don Teobaldo, he added:

"Pull out one of the hairs of my mane and keep it in your pocket, with this you will have as much power as I. Try to defend yourself to the last, for our adversary is terrible."

No sooner said than done. Don Teobaldo pulled out one of the hairs of the devil's mane and kept it, and immediately felt strong and powerful. Blinded by all the pride of the Infernal One, he assailed the knight of the white armor, trying to fascinate him with his shield. Useless task!

The knight raised the visor of his helmet and showed the handsomest countenance that ever was seen. That lovely face sent out celestial rays.

"Ah, Luzbel!" cried he. "Do you rebel against me?"

And, throwing aside his spear, he drew his sword, whose brilliance eclipsed that of the sun itself, and threw himself upon Don Teobaldo. The black horse snorted, roared, bounded, evading the blows with superhuman skill. Don Teobaldo's sword fell upon Miguel's white shield two hundred times, but

---

7   An ermine is a white, short-haired weasel, also known as a stoat.

in vain, until dazed and vanquished horse and rider fell at the feet of the handsome knight.

"Get you hence!" he said in a voice of infinite pity. "Know that you are my slave until the completion of the centuries, and that you have no power against God our Lord."

"Princess," he added, "you are saved. Your prayer reached the Most High, and I, who am the Archangel Miguel, came to set you free from the snares of the demon. Continue virtuous and you will receive your reward."

And so saying he disappeared.

Meanwhile the devil wished to vanish, but Don Teobaldo remembered his deceit, and as he had power over the demon, thanks to the hair that he had pulled out, began to belabor him with spurs and sword, making him bounce as high as the highest houses. Don Teobaldo did not move from the saddle and finished by giving the devil such a superb thrashing as nearly finished him.

"Let me be, and I will not trouble you again," cried Luzbel.

"Will you ask for my soul?"

"Neither your soul nor your body, but let me alone now."

Then Don Teobaldo, whose heart had been touched by the glance of the angel and moved to repentance, dismounted from the horse and left it free to disappear.

And so ended those famous jousts, which were never eradicated from the memory of the public.

The princess, the following year, married a prince as virtuous as herself, and Don Teobaldo did penance and became a good Christian who had a just satisfaction in having administered a sound thrashing to the devil.

THE TREASURE OF THE DRAGON

An old sailor brought to my town the news of having seen, in a very distant island, a terrible dragon which guarded an immense treasure. Half of the body of this guardian was a fish, the other half a lion; it moreover had such powerful wings that it could rise to an extraordinary height. Air, water, or land were his elements, and when any ships came near to the coast they were soon attacked by that ever vigilant monster.

Many expeditions were made, but all succumbed to the talons of that invincible animal; moreover, the treasure was so splendid that it excited the envy of adventurers from all parts of the earth.

Among the innumerable precious stones which with thousands of gold bars formed those riches, there was a statue of natural size made out of a single diamond, and which was worth such a fabulous sum that all the treasures of the earth would not suffice to buy it.

The fear of the dragon did not lessen the enthusiasm of the lads of my town; on the contrary, it was a further stimulus to their bravery and daring, and so, in little less than a month, an expedition was formed of the bravest and most ambitious.

They set out on the 15th of September on a bark named the *Temeraire*—a handsome brigantine, the swiftest that ever glided over the waves. After fourteen days' sailing they found themselves at about a league from the island where the treasure and the dragon were. Behold what happened!

The members of the expedition met in council in order to take their measures, and agreed as follows: to launch some boats in order to land in three or four places at the same time;

to carry a great quantity of ammunition so as to be able to fire upon the dragon; and, lastly, to divide the treasure in equal parts and to distribute it among the expeditionaries. There was only one vote against, that of a cabin boy, a youth of eighteen, who opposed the dividing of the party, believing it better to wait for the dragon on board the ship, and from there to fight it with cannons.

"If you are afraid, stay behind," they all said to him, and nobody paid any attention to the cabin boy's scheme.

As nobody trusted his companions, all embarked in the bunches, fearful of being cheated if they did not witness the division of the treasure, leaving on board only the cabin boy and the pilot, a very experienced old sailor who had not uttered any opinion at the meeting. The launches being full and the crews armed, they left the ship and rowed near to the coast.

Pascual, for so the cabin boy was named, prepared the bow-gun, loading it up to the mouth, and also seized a strong sharp spear. Then he sat down in the bows, and from there, with a telescope, watched the progress of his companions. The latter were about a hundred yards from the coast when a tremendous roar was heard; he saw the dragon fly up into the air and fall upon one of the launches. Several gunshots were heard, and soon the launch disappeared under the water. The bullets glanced off the skin of the terrible animal, which threw itself in turn upon the other launches and sank them.

Its work of extermination finished, the dragon returned to the island, shaking its wings, reddened by the blood of its victims.

The pilot, terrified, wished to go back to his country, but Pascual prevented it, and directed him to go at full sail towards the island.

The pilot gave way to the solicitations of the cabin boy, who now no longer thought of the treasure but of avenging the death of his companions.

They had arrived at some hundred fathoms from the coast when they saw the dragon, which was advancing towards them. Pascual rapidly aimed the small cannon, but the ball struck on some rocks, and the dragon, more irritated than ever, threw himself upon the brigantine. It described a couple of circles in the air like an eagle choosing its prey, and at length threw itself upon Pascual, who, mounted on a round house, valiantly waited for it.

Such was the violence of the attack that the dragon, on attempting to break the spear with which the heroic boy greeted it, sent it quite through one of its claws, and so great was the pain that it made a horrible outcry and rose up in the air full of terrible frenzy. The spear remained fixed in the claw, and to it hung Pascual, who, by his weight, increased the woes of the dragon. In vain the latter tried to get rid of that singular guest; all its efforts were useless, Pascual bestrode his spear like an enthusiastic gymnast. Then becoming furious, it threw itself into the sea in order to try to drown him. Pascual swam like a fish and dived like a seal; so his enemy was not able to liberate itself from him. Being now desperate, it went to the island, dragging the cabin boy with it; the latter had hardly touched terra firma when, using the spear as a lever, he gave it a turn with all his might, twisting the wounded claw in such a way that the pain deprived the monster of its strength and consciousness. Giving a cry it fell to the ground defenceless. Pascual then got out his jack-knife and looked with care for the joints between the formidable scales which served the dragon as armor. There he thrust it in many times, with the aid of a stone which he used in place of a hammer.

The dragon was now dead, and Pascual thought of his companions and went down to the shore to seek them. His search was useless, for he did not even find a trace of them. He looked towards the spot where he had left the brigantine, and that had also disappeared; doubtless the old pilot was afraid and had gone away with the ship.

Then our hero decided to seek the treasure, but in vain he went over the island in all directions: he found not the least sign of it. Then he returned to the spot where he had seen the dragon lying when they had approached the island, and he saw that there was an enormous stone which no doubt covered the entrance of the grotto where the treasure was to be found. He applied the spear to the joints and succeeded in moving it, and after some effort he brought into view a winding staircase, down which he hurriedly went. The first room to which the staircase gave access had its walls covered with rubies, the second with emeralds, and the third with pearls and diamonds. In the centre stood the magnificent statue made out of a single diamond, and which represented a very beautiful princess. Pascual was astounded at such extraordinary beauty, and burst into an exclamation of admiration.

Presently he noticed the pedestal of the statue, on which might be read:

"In a stone lies the disenchantment."

Then the cabin boy looked at all the projections of the room, and pressing one of them heard a creak, and instantaneously, as the scenes in a fairy comedy are changed, the grotto disappeared; each precious stone was changed into a human being, and the beautiful princess, again turned to flesh and blood, came slowly down from her pedestal, and, giving her hand to the valiant lad, offered to reward his bravery by giving him all the riches of her kingdom, and with them her heart. Among the disenchanted beings were all his companions of the expedition, who embraced Pascual, and, what was very strange, did not envy him, recognising that his triumph was deserved. All the destroyed boats appeared on the coast, and in them they embarked, each one going to his own country and the cabin boy to that of the princess.

Pascual is now no longer Pascual, but His Highness Prince Pascual I, a very good man, according to what his subjects say.

THE MAN WITH THE
TWO FACES

Claudio was screaming madly when his grandmother said to him:

"If you cry any more you will see the man with two faces."

"Oh, I say, who is he?"

"Well, he is a very strange being, who laughs with one face and cries with the other. If a child looks at his smiling face he gives it a toy; if it looks at his sad face he bites it and tears off the tip of his ear."

"Well, then, I wish he would come, because I will be very good and he will give me a toy."

"It would be much better if he did not come, because you are very bad and you would get your ear bitten."

"But I want to see him," said the boy.

"Look for him if you like," said the grandmother, "but mind he does not hurt you."

Claudio, who was eight years old and very innocent, quite believed in the man with two faces, and resolved to look for him everywhere.

That afternoon he went to the outskirts of the town and asked some woodmen:

"Where is the man with two faces?"

And they said to him mockingly:

"Go to the mountain over there and you will come to him."

He followed their counsel and climbed up the mountain without finding anybody. That night he had to spend on the mountain, climbing up to the top of a tree because the howling of the wolves frightened him so much that he did not dare to go back to his home. In the morning, on getting down from the tree, a squirrel saluted him with great ceremony, and said "Good morning."

"Listen, squirrel," said Claudio, "do you know where the man with two faces is?"

"I do not know, but my friend the eagle knows many things. Come with me and we will ask him."

The boy and the squirrel went together and on the topmost part of the mountain came upon the eagle's nest. The eagle turned towards the squirrel and asked what he wanted. On being told of what Claudio wanted he said to him: "I have sometimes heard this man spoken of, but I have never seen him. I only know that he is very unhappy, because he can only look at himself in the glass with his sad face, and on seeing himself so afflicted the poor fellow bursts into tears."

"And where does he live?" said the boy.

"He lives so far away that you would never be able to reach the place, but if you like I will carry you there, through the air, in my claws, and we shall be there in a twinkling. I cannot do any more for you than carry you to the door of his house, and I cannot answer for what may happen to you."

"Never mind," said the boy; "take me, for I want to see him."

The eagle caught up the boy by his belt and the squirrel got into one of Claudio's pockets. The eagle began its flight and the three found themselves in the air. When Claudio saw that he was so high up he shut his eyes, full of terror.

When the squirrel appeared from the boy's pocket the trees looked like the size of pins, and he went quickly back again for fear of being seasick. After several hours' flying, the eagle descended on a little mountain and there left Claudio, startled at his own temerity.

"When you wish to come back—if they let you—blow on the whistle which I am carrying round my neck. Keep it, for I have very sharp ears and can hear the sound of it for five hundred leagues. As soon as I hear it I will come, and pop! I will take you by the belt to my nest."

When the eagle had gone the squirrel came out of Claudio's pocket and said to him:

"Have we arrived already, my little friend?"

"Have you come too?" exclaimed Claudio joyfully.

"Yes, but incognito. I liked the look of you and wish to help you with my advice: you know that squirrels, modesty apart, are very sharp."

"All right, what am I going to do now?"

"Do you not want to see this man? Then let us go on, because I also would like to know him."

"And if he wants to hurt us?"

"Then we will defend ourselves. I will go first and explore the surroundings, and will come back at once."

And saying this, the squirrel started to run with the quickness usual to his race, returning after a little while very much frightened.

"Do you know," he said, "that the man with the two faces is at the present moment giving a terrible hiding to some boys that he has shut up in a cage?"

"They must be naughty boys, but I am good, and he will give me toys."

"I don't know about that, because the only thing I have seen him give is knocks; and do you know what he was saying?

"This one I like, that one, no;

But I shall kill them all, O!'"

"Was he saying that?"

"Just what I am telling you. I have only seen his gay face which is in the back of his head, and on seeing him I closed my eyes and came away quickly, for if he sees me he will tear me to bits."

"What are we going to do?" said Claudio, startled.

"Climb up this pine tree with me and from there we will watch."

They climbed up a tree and from it saw a house, or rather a great cage, formed of big iron bars with an iron roof. In the centre was seated the man with the two faces with a whip in his hand, punishing a number of boys of all ages who filled the cage.

The temptation seized Claudio to blow the whistle and make the eagle come back to fetch him away, but his curiosity overcame his fear, and he said to himself:

"After all, I can go away whenever I like."

A little later they saw the man with two faces come out of the cage and walk in the direction of the place where Claudio was. On his approach they saw such a woebegone countenance that Claudio was filled with fear. As the squirrel saw him shudder, he said to him in a very low voice:

"Close your eyes or we are lost."

The boy obeyed and the man with two faces passed close to them without noticing their presence. When he felt him pass, Claudio half opened his eyes and saw his gay face. Again he had to close them, for he could hardly stop laughing, so strange was the face.

On his disappearing in the distance, both the friends

descended from the tree and went up to the cage. On seeing them the boy prisoners began to shout, full of joy:

"Have you come to set us free?"

"Yes," said Claudio, "but I don't know how to, because you are locked up. Well, failing the key, let us look for other means."

And, examining the doors, he came upon one without a lock. He opened it and went into the cage, but he had no sooner entered than the door closed of its own accord, leaving him a prisoner.

"Poor little boy!" shouted the others, "you are quite lost, for this is a kind of mouse-trap where you can enter but can't get out."

At this moment, the man with two faces arrived; he opened the door and, facing Claudio, looked at him with the serious face which made the boy shut his eyes to keep from crying.

"What! Have I got one pupil more?" he exclaimed. "Good, now it is your turn to laugh, as it is the first day."

And seizing his head with both hands he turned it round so that the gay face came in front of the boy. The latter looked a moment, and again shut his eyes to keep from laughing aloud.

"I see that you are strong, but tomorrow we shall see," said the monster, and he locked Claudio up with the other little ones.

Now it was night; all were sleeping, including the horrible gaoler.

Claudio was half asleep when he heard himself called softly. It was his friend the squirrel, who had got in through the iron bars and said to him:

"Be sure that tomorrow I will save you."

And without anything more he turned and went out by the way he had entered.

The following day, at the usual time, the monster showed his sad face. The prisoners began to cry. Claudio shut his eyes, and the monster gave one of his ears a bite and showed him his teeth.

"That's for today; tomorrow there will be more," he said.

And after throwing a few pieces of bread to the boys he went away.

No sooner had he gone than millions of squirrels gathered round, and with the quickness of lightning made an enormous gap. Through this the boys escaped, and the squirrels entered in their place. The boys hid themselves in a distant grotto, and there waited to see what would happen.

The man with the two faces arrived at the cage and, on seeing the squirrels there, became extremely angry, and seized a whip with which to give them the daily beating, when all those little animals came out through the iron bars.

The monster, putting on some very high stilts, started to run in search of the boys, blowing a whistle. They, terror-stricken, were hiding in the grotto without daring to breathe for fear of being discovered. After eight or ten hours of giddy running, the man with the two faces fell down exhausted and went to sleep on the ground near the grotto. Then the squirrel asked Claudio for the whistle that the eagle had given him, and without making any noise hung it round the monster's neck.

Then the latter, awakened by the cold of the night, again caught hold of the whistle and started to blow it madly. The eagle hastened to the sound of his whistle, and thinking that it was Claudio, seized the man with the two faces in his claws and rose up to a great height.

The eagle soon noticed that his voice was unknown, and without more ado let go of his load and the monster was dashed to pieces on the rocks below.

He flew again towards the place where he had left Claudio.

"Don't be afraid," said the eagle, "because of the two faces neither remains. They have just been smashed up against the stones, and he will never torment anybody any more."

The children returned to their homes, where their coming was celebrated with great feasts, and Claudio's grandmother, when she heard what had happened, after welcoming him on his return, only said to him:

"Do you want to see the man with two faces again?"

THE TREACHERY OF MICIFUF

Rather more than a fortnight ago an importunate guest disturbed my quiet and would not leave me in peace during those tranquil hours of the night which I am accustomed to spend in work.

You will say that I ought to have got rid of him. Nothing more simple, apparently, than to seize the disturbing guest and to put him on his feet in the street, saying to him: "Good friend, do me the favor not to come back to this house while I live in it and while you behave so badly."

But with my guest there is no reasoning at all. I begged him, with the most delicate phrases from the book of courtesy, to go away, or not to make a noise. On seeing his insistence, I reached, by degrees, from the simple threat of dismissal to the terrible one (it frightens me to remember!) of dealing him a vile and treacherous death. To such a point does hastiness on occasions blind us! Even to crime!

And to any one in the same circumstances I suspect the same thing would occur.

Because what he does is so irritating. At the moment when I compose myself for writing, at that very moment he makes an unbearable noise that gets on my nerves and prevents me from writing calmly a single line, and from even putting together my ideas. When, tired of the torture, I throw down my pen and go to bed, the mocking noise at once ceases as if by magic, and the silence of the dead, or of those who work, reigns again in my room.

But there is still more! As I leave them scattered on the table, my poor papers appear the following morning as if they were the remains of a kite, crumpled and even torn, turning my writing to strange hieroglyphics, incapable of being read, and my books, my poor books, which are so dear to me, they are cut as if with a saw, covers and all!

Such an enemy well deserved the tremendous punishment which my legitimate indignation prepared for him. I maintain him, but he, however, illtreats me! Have you ever seen such black ingratitude?

So I spoke to several friends of mine not long ago, and finding my pacific and easy-going nature so changed to such a decided and determined attitude, and to such a fixed project of sanguinary vengeance, they said to me, quite surprised and bewildered:

"We did not believe you capable of such thoughts! To assassinate! to avenge! When, even in extreme cases, it might be legitimate and honorable it leaves a stain in the mouth and in the mind of him who thinks it. We do not understand you now, my friend; with such principles one goes to prison or to the scaffold with surprising ease. If it is an ingrate who is to be dealt with, turn him ignominiously out of your house and leave him alone."

And I noticed in my audience a movement of repulsion that made me feel uneasy.

"But now it occurs to me that I have spoken," I added, "without telling who is the person concerned. It is a mouse which, hidden behind my bookcase, makes an infernal noise about twelve o'clock at night, the hour at which I dedicate myself to my work. It is he who destroys everything within the reach of his nails or teeth, who must have in his body more letters than a printing press and more paper than a paper-mill."

Either it was an old and seasoned mouse, experienced

in malicious tricks, or what he has gnawed has taught him to be on his guard against everything. Be that as it may, it is certain that there is no instrument, mouse-trap, or poison which could put the wretch to death and ensure my tranquility.

You ought to have seen me some nights handling an old cavalry sabre, pursuing the little mouse, which finished by hiding itself between the bookcase and the wall, laughing at my cutting and thrusting.

Convinced that there was nothing to be done against such an agile enemy, I called to my aid a cat who was well known for his courage and hatred of the mouse tribe, big Micifuf, who, although old and retired from active life, had no objection to placing himself at my disposal, only on certain fixed conditions.

"If you want me to help you," he said to me, "you must entertain me like a prince; must buy me a fine gilt collar; and when I have killed the mouse who troubles you, must make me a good present for my family."

I agreed to all this, provided I was freed of the diabolical creature and in the belief that that same night it would fall into the power of my ally.

After a little time I noticed that the noise disappeared, which was something of a consolation, and I observed that the good Micifuf was lying near the bookcase. He looked at me and smiled as if to say, "There, you see! as soon as they smell me about all is over."

I do not Know whether it was instinct or suspicion: it is certain and true that I thought a certain understanding existed between the mouse and Micifuf, and decided to spy upon them to convince myself of this treachery.

"The mouse does not come out," I said to myself, "and

if he does not come out from behind the bookcase for these three or four days and has not eaten anything all this time, the unhappy creature must be on the point of dying of hunger, if it is not already dead. Well, then, if it is alive there is doubtless some trickery here!"

A few days afterwards I overheard a long conversation between Micifuf and the mouse.

Said the former to the latter: "Now you see I don't interfere with you at all. On the contrary, I myself supply you with food, giving it to you on the sly as we agreed. But if you make a noise I shall be obliged to lay hands on you, in which case, frankly, neither you nor I would derive any benefit—you, because you run the risk of my devouring you at a mouthful; and I because, once you are dead, the master would send me away, and I shall not be able to find another fool like this, who keeps me and treats me famously without my doing any work whatever."

"For my part," said the mouse, "I don't think I shall break the compact. I don't move, even to sneeze; so that you ought to be very pleased. By the way, you might be good enough to increase my rations of cheese, for you know I like it immensely, and above all Gruyère[8]."

At this moment I could not restrain my indignation, and calling Micifuf I said to him:

"You are a cat without honor; what you have done is a really dirty trick of the worst kind. I should never have brought you here for that purpose, for I could have made an arrangement with the mouse myself. I prefer to keep him rather than to feed you both."

"Come, come!" exclaimed Micifuf with the utmost cool-

8   Gruyère is a type of cheese, from the town of Gruyères in Switzerland.

ness. "I see you have not understood my plan. Listen! By acting so with the mouse, which is an unhappy creature in the fullest sense of the word, I shall succeed in getting him out of his haunts, and he will yield himself trustingly to my claws and teeth."

So that very night he approached the bookcase and said:

"Little mouse, my friend! Come out, for now nobody is about and we can chat at our ease."

The mouse showed its little snout from behind the bookcase and came out, little by little, with justifiable fear.

"Come now, draw near, and don't make me raise my voice, I don't know whether they can hear us. Listen to what I have to tell you. You must know, my good friend, that I have always felt a great affection for your race, by reason of a tradition which has been preserved in my family for many years. According to this, one of our ancestors, a beautiful Angora cat—I don't know exactly whether it was my great-grandfather or my great-great-grandfather—was once very ill and without resources, lying on the miserable straw of a garret, when a compassionate mouse brought him some cheese-rinds and, I suppose, some other eatables right up to his own bed. He was going to take them when another mouse, of disagreeable appearance, with some red marks on its back, drew near and took away the food, taking advantage of the fact that my great-grandfather had rheumatism and could not move.

"Since then we have decided to kill all the descendants of that wicked fellow who made our relative die of hunger, and also to reward the one who was so good to him in time of trouble."

"That appears quite right to me," said the mouse.

"Listen, by the by: do you know it seems to me that you

have some red spots on your back?"

The mouse was startled and said that his good friend the cat must have cobwebs in his eyes.

"Really, I am very shortsighted, and it would not be at all extraordinary if I were mistaken. I will come near in order to recognise you better."

He had no sooner approached than, seizing him with his claws, he began to shout:

"Master! Master! Here is the mouse!"

I hastened at the call, and, if the truth must be told, far from being pleased, the deed troubled me in the highest degree.

The little mouse lay dead in Micifuf's claws, and the cat was showing himself off, proud of his achievement.

"I hope," said he, "that you will give me the reward agreed on."

Then I could no longer restrain my indignation, and, seizing a stick, I began to whack the traitor, saying to him:

"Wretch! At first you would have deceived me, and now, by practising the wiles of traitors, you have murdered him to whom you offered protection. Take the reward which all traitors receive."

At each blow with the stick Micifuf snorted, leaping high into the air, until at length he dashed through a pane of the window and threw himself out into the street. I did not wish to know whether he was killed or not. He well deserved to be killed.

And since then, everybody who has recourse to deceit seems hateful to me, even though they deceive for the purpose of killing the most troublesome of little mice.

TROMPETILLA AND TROMPETIN

"What are you doing here, boy?" asked a venerable friar of Rupert, who was sitting near his accordion in the neighborhood of a wood as if he were preparing himself to give a solemn performance to the oaks.

"I was resting after a long walk," answered the boy, "and as they say that sleep is food, I wished to forget in slumber that not a mouthful has passed my lips for many hours."

"Poor little boy," exclaimed the father; "if you want a sumptuous meal go near the third cork-tree on the right-hand side; go round the tree three times, playing the accordion, and a door will open. Pass through it and you shall eat splendidly."

Rupert went to the spot indicated and, playing a "Habanera" dance, made the three turns prescribed; a piece of bark came away and disclosed a little iron door, artistically ornamented. He pushed it gently; it opened noiselessly, and there was Rupert inside a beautiful palace, whose magnificent rooms were illuminated with hidden fires, which, while giving light, sent out sweet fragrance. "These smells are not bad," said Rupert, "but I would rather they came from a nicely cooked chop."

At that moment a hundred succulent chops which were saying "Eat me!" began to balance themselves in space. Being neither stupid nor lazy, Rupert tried to get hold of the nearest, but they all began a frantic career round the room. In the centre of the latter appeared a table covered with appetising eatables, but as soon as Rupert went near they once more took to flight as if on invisible wings. A magnificent stuffed turkey hit him on the nose; the breast of a chicken nearly knocked him over; all this while the boy was running, like a mad thing, after those exquisite dainties, hungrier than a bear after a fortnight's fast.

"This is only an invitation to see!" exclaimed the lad. "It is enough to make one's teeth grow longer!"

He had hardly uttered these words than his teeth began to grow in such a disordered fashion, and so quickly, that the shortest was not less than three yards long. The viands were caught on them as if on lances, a further difficulty for Rupert, who could not succeed in seizing the coveted prey which was fixed on his own teeth.

On this a monkey appeared, and climbing on to the boy's teeth, began very impudently to eat those exquisite viands, making signs of satisfaction which threw Rupert into a rage.

"You great thief!" he cried. "What do you mean by laughing at me?"

And catching up his accordion he threw it at the animal with such accuracy that, hitting him on the head, it knocked him senseless. A great noise was heard, the monkey disappeared, Rupert's teeth grew shorter, and while the accordion played, of its own accord, the celebrated air "No me matas," a woman appeared in the middle of the room who, for size, looked like a whale, and who would have been beautiful if she had not had a turned-up nose and fixed eyes, one weeping oil and the other vinegar, and who would certainly have had a fine head of hair if she had not been bald, and a fine set of teeth if a single tooth had remained in her head.

"Who are you?" asked Rupert, a trifle startled.

"I am the witch Trompetilla, the daughter of the celebrated Trompeton and grand-daughter of Trompetazo, and am looking for my son Trompetin everywhere, without being able to find him."

"Why do you speak to me about Trompetilla and Trompetin when I never played a trumpet in my life?"

"Ah, unhappy me!" sobbed the witch. "In vain I have offered a pennyworth of toasted chick peas and a measure of tiger nuts to the mortal who discovers the whereabouts of my son. I have wept so much oil and vinegar that I have spoilt all the furniture in my house."

"What a fine salad you could make if you bought some lettuces!"

"You will get a salad made of blows if you don't help me to look for my Trompetin, and if we find him I will invite you to supper, and moreover will give you a penny so that you need never do any more work in your life."

Roused by such a magnificent promise, Rupert offered to look for Trompetin, even if he were under a cruet.

"What is he like?" he asked.

"The size of a pea, a head like that of a pin, and legs like needles."

"Well, then, he must be sticking in a pin cushion or in a needle-case."

"A needle-case would not hold him, for he has a beard two yards long."

"It must trail on the ground!" said Rupert, full of astonishment.

"Well, now," said the witch, "while I go and mend some clothes, begin to look for my pet."

This said, she disappeared.

The boy was confused by so many comings and goings, appearances and disappearances; but as hunger afflicted him, he proposed to find Trompetin, and taking a turn round the room, began to shout:

"Trompetin, where are you?"

"Here!" groaned a tiny voice.

"Where? I can't see you."

"In this crack," replied the voice.

Rupert searched, and at last found the witch's son in a crack between two bricks. The enormous beard was a hair two yards long, which grew out of his nose.

Rupert took him up carefully, and placing him on his hand, asked him:

"Are you Trompetin, the son of Trompetilla?"

"The same."

"Why have you been lost so long?"

"Because my mother is deaf and cannot see well, so that, although I shouted a lot, she did not hear me."

"Well, now, tell me who the monkey is that climbed up on to my teeth?"

"It is a wizard, nastier than medicine, who is angry with us because his grandfather died from a trumpet-blast that my great-great-grandfather sounded in his ear. It was he who made your teeth grow, and didn't allow you to eat. Knock on this wall and he will reappear, then pull out my hair and thrash him with it."

"A fine thrashing to be given with a hair!"

"Try, and you will see!"

Rupert struck the wall, and at once the monkey appeared, sparks flying from his eyes. He was about to throw himself on Rupert, but the boy pulled out Trompetin's hair, which turned itself into a fine cudgel, with which he dealt the monkey a vigorous hiding. The animal leapt high into the air several times, but that was useless, as the stick lengthened as if it were elastic and reached him wherever he was. When the monkey could resist no longer, he took human shape, and going on his knees begged Rupert not to grind his ribs, and in return he offered to give him as much wealth as he might desire.

"Call Trompetilla," exclaimed the lad, "and let us have a talk."

The witch appeared, this time crying with joy at seeing her son, and after kissing him, stuck him in her dress so that he should not be lost again. The wizard gave Rupert a lot of money and the witch gave him a splendid supper of stew and hemp-seed.

When supper was over they affectionately took leave of one another, and the wizard took Rupert out into the fresh air, carrying him carefully to the same spot in which he was when he met the priest. There he left the boy sleeping soundly, dreaming of a sweet awakening—the dream of the person who sees his future assured by reason of not having done anything wrong.

THE QUACK DOCTOR

I do not know whether it was true or not, but as it was told to me so I tell it to you.

There used to pass through the goodly streets, whether of Constantinople[9] or Babylon[10] I am not sure which—however, it makes no difference to my story—a quack doctor who, while beating a drum and clashing a pair of cymbals, announced his medicines and practised his cures.

You must place the action of this story in a place where there are no medical men, for if there were, certainly they would put the quack in prison where he would not see daylight for a long time. And the fact is that, with all his quackery, the man had acquired great fame in the difficult art to which he devoted himself. His adaptability was extraordinary. It was just the same to him to extract a big man's tooth as to pull out a knife and cut off anybody's leg without stopping for a moment.

For shamelessness this man could not be beaten. It is related that in the times when our quack wandered through the streets and towns, the emperor's son fell ill of a great and persistent melancholy. The youth was sad and weak, and even when he felt no pain his depression was alarming. The court doctors, who were important people, held a consultation, and, as always happens in these cases, each one put forward a different opinion from that of his companions.

"It appears to me," said one, putting on his spectacles, "saving the estimable opinion of my fellow-professors, that

9   Constantinople (present-day Istanbul in Turkey) was the capital of the Byzantine Empire.
10   The Kingdom of Babylon was located in Mesopotamia, the capital of which was located in present-day Iraq.

his highness the hereditary prince is suffering from his liver. Broth of green beans would be a good thing."

"Gently, wise companion," exclaimed another. "I maintain that his highness suffers from his spleen; and as what is good for the liver is bad for the other organ, I do not believe that green beans would be any good; roasted chick peas are wanted."

"Well, gentlemen, may I be hanged if the prince's illness is not in his feet. Ask him if he has chilblains, and, in that case, we all know what to do: wool, plenty of wool, and watercress, plenty of watercress."

The discussion took a threatening turn; each doctor, in support of what he affirmed, cited three or four authorities and even brought books to prove and demonstrate it. The dispute waxed so hot that it ended by the doctors throwing the books at each other's heads. A book broke the spectacles of one of the doctors, and a little more would have knocked out one of his eyes; another fell like a mace on the bald head of the oldest and crashed into his brain, his skull not being of the hardest.

At this moment the emperor entered the room where the three Hippocrates were killing each other, and when informed of the cause of the dispute became cold all over.

"It is a bad sign when you do not agree. My son is in danger of dying."

And the poor father went away, saddened and disheartened, to his apartments.

History says that not a bit of the doctors remained. On seeing the emperor so grief-stricken there was no lack of courtiers who had the courage to speak to him of the advisibility of calling in the quack.

"Impossible," said the monarch. "If those three shining lights of medicine could not save him, how can I possibly expect that the quack can cure him?"

However, the courtiers were so persistent that the emperor consented to call in the quack, but on one condition: before taking up the cure of the prince, he must heal five sick people who had been given up by the doctors.

They looked for the five invalids and had them brought into the palace. The quack, obeying the emperor's orders, arrived shortly after. The latter said to him:

"Do you dare to undertake the prince's cure?"

"Yes, sire."

"Well, in order to convince me of what you know, you will heal five men who are seriously ill and whom I will show you. If you do not cure them I will have your head cut off, but if you make them well I will thenceforward put his highness' health in your charge."

"Can you not make it four instead of five, sire?"

"No, five; and if not, you know what to expect."

"Well, then, I will cure them. Where are they? I must speak to them alone."

With the emperor's permission he went to the room where the hopeless cases were. Even the most healthy of them had only two or three days to live.

On seeing them our quack almost fell in a faint.

"Gentlemen," he said, "I am going to cure you in the only possible way. The great magician Faramalla has taught me a wonderful system of curing. There is no invalid who cannot be healed by it. Hear it:

"It is necessary for me to kill one of you and burn his heart. Its ashes serve to make such a pomade that on applying it to any diseased part it heals as if by magic, without any need of medicine. You," he added, facing one of the hopeless ones, "are very ill, what does it matter to you if you die now or within two days? I shall kill you and burn your heart to cinders in order to cure the rest."

"I say, good friend," cried the threatened man, "do you say I am very ill? Why, there is nothing the matter with me. My family persists in saying that I am consumptive, but, thank God, I am as sound as a bell."

"All right, all right," said the quack, "it makes very little difference to me; but you leave on this condition, that you tell the emperor that you are cured."

The consumptive, hardly noticing the half-opened door, dashed madly homewards.

"How are you?" the emperor asked him.

"I am sound and well," exclaimed the consumptive, without ceasing to run.

"This is marvellous," thought the emperor.

"He is a very learned man," said the courtiers.

The other invalids did the same as the first. Provided that they were not killed at once, they swore by all they held sacred that they had never felt stronger and better in their lives. And they darted out of the palace like arrows from a bow, leaving the emperor and the doctors amazed.

The monarch then thought of trusting him with the cure of his son, when a loud burst of laughter interrupted the grave and ceremonious etiquette of the court. Who was the daring man who thus failed in due respect?

The emperor in person, full of ire, went out into the ante-room and there met the disturber. It was the imperial prince himself, who was rolling on a sofa unable to restrain his outbursts of laughter. The emperor was delighted to see the sadness, which had so alarmed him, dissipated so unexpectedly. To what was this extraordinary event due?

The prince told him. "On seeing those unhappy invalids run out so quickly, I asked the quack the cause of their flight, and the latter told me with a wealth of detail."

It had amused him so much that the black melancholy which was undermining his existence was dissipated.

"You will remain with my son," said the emperor to the quack, "not as a doctor but as a friend. You are a witty man and wit deserves to be rewarded."

THE DRAWING SCHOOL

Once there was a boy so fond of spoiling walls, doors, and windows with grotesque drawings that there was no way of stopping him from practising his silly cleverness wherever he was. And I say silly, because from his hand came forth some primitive dolls, with heads as round as a billiard ball, eyes and nose forming a sort of cork, and arms and legs like thin thread, terminating in hands and feet which required an inscription in order not to be taken for scourges.

One afternoon he approached the very wall of the school, and there, with the greatest coolness, commenced to draw with a piece of charcoal some of his strange figures. Perico, for so the boy was called, traced the figure of the head of a puppet, made the eyes and the mouth, and, oh, how strange! the doll began to wink and open its mouth and put its tongue out like anything.

Perico was not timid, and therefore the moving of the eyes and mouth did not startle him, and so without paying attention continued with his sketching the arms and the rest of the body. But he had hardly finished when the doll's hand came out and gave him such a tremendous knock that it made him lose his balance, and he would even have fallen to the ground if another blow with the other hand and on the opposite cheek had not kept him on his feet. And as if this was not enough, the legs sprang out of the wall, and two vigorous kicks that Perico received in the pit of the stomach quite convinced him that there was one too many, and he was the one. Thus convinced he was about to run away when the whole doll came away from the stone, and at a bound leapt on his shoulders and began to bite him in the back of the head.

Perico ran towards his house like a greyhound, feeling on his neck the weight of that unexpected load, when the latter grew heavy, as if, instead of a charcoal picture, he had to deal with a bronze statue.

The poor little boy sank to the ground, and on getting up saw at his side, in the middle of the square, the doll in question, as tall as a giant and changed into a motionless iron statue.

He tried to fly, but the statue caught him with its great hands by the neck and, raising him up, placed him on its shoulders, and this being done commenced to run in the direction of the country. Its footsteps produced a very disagreeable noise of ironmongery, something like a sack of nails being shaken up.

It was night-time and our giant, with Perico on its shoulders, ran as fast as anything to a neighboring mountain, until he came to a dark grotto into which he penetrated without any need of matches, because intense lights shone from his eyes.

During all this Perico, needless to mention, was more afraid than ashamed, and did not know, nor could even imagine how, it was going to end.

At length, after some minutes' walk in the grotto, the iron man straightened himself, and turning the light of his eyes towards a corner, lighted up by a glance the lamp which hung down from the rocky ceiling, and this being done, took Perico down from his shoulders and sat down.

"You do not know who I am," said the doll, opening his mouth with a horrible smile; "but when you do know, it will make your hair stand on end from fright."

"I am sure it won't," said the lad, "because it is already doing so; and as I cannot be any more afraid than I am now, on account of being so much afraid the fear which I felt is passing away."

"Well, then, I am the magician Adefesio, and I am tired of your drawing me so ugly and so similar to all the boys. The thing which puts me out most is that you draw my eyes without pupils and my nose without nostrils. Moreover, the ears which you sketch look like jug handles, and I am sick of my portrait going about the world so disfigured and so badly done. Could you not have learnt to draw a little before commencing these pictures? Well, the punishment that I reserve for you is to draw your portrait every day."

"What a punishment!" exclaimed Perico.

"The fact is that I do not know how to draw either," answered the man of iron, "and the worst of it all is that while I am drawing you, you will grow like my sketch, so that in a twinkling you will be disfigured. There, does not that seem a severe punishment to you? Well, you will see!"

And seizing Perico by one arm he pulled the lamp which hung down. Then a hole opened in the ceiling and the lamp went up, dragging the doll and Perico through the air.

The light continued to rise through a sort of well which was lighted up, and whose walls were lined with books full of badly-made drawings, spoilt plans, pieces of forms with engravings made with penknives, and table-covers destroyed through having been drawn on. That was the museum of the man of iron, and each time he saw it he was filled with anger towards the young draughtsmen who spoilt everything.

Soon they found themselves in a spacious room decorated in Arabian style and furnished most luxuriously. In the background there was an easel of great size, and on it a blackboard on which were drawn a lot of dolls of the same sort that

Perico drew.

"Dear me, how fine!" said the boy looking at the sketches; "it seems that I did them."

"Well, now you will see the consequences," and snapping his fingers he produced a metallic sound, and immediately a multitude of boys of different ages came through a door. But what funny boys! All had round heads, eyes like fishes, flat noses, and mouths like letter boxes, wide open and showing teeth like saws. Their arms were thin as wire, ending in long fingers without joints. Perico was not startled when they came in.

"Well, that is how you will look in a little while," said the iron man.

"He always exaggerates!" exclaimed Perico aside, "but seeing is believing."

The man of iron seized a piece of chalk, and going near to the board began to draw Perico's head; but the latter called the doll's attention, and when he looked the other way rubbed out what he had drawn.

The man could not have seen very well because he went on drawing very tranquilly, and Perico continued rubbing out what the other drew; and when he thought that he had finished he caught up the boy, brought him to the light, and imagine his surprise on seeing him the same as before. He went back, full of rage, to the blackboard; but Perico tripped him up, and did it so well that he fell down. Then he threw the board and easel on him, and climbing on top, began to jump on the doll, and calling to his companions, shouted:

"Come here so that he will not be able to run away!"

The boys drew near and, climbing on the blackboard, by their weight prevented the iron doll from moving.

But things did not rest thus, because Perico was a very daring boy, and taking up a rope, which was close at hand, hung the iron man by the neck to the lamp, and pulling on the other end of the rope, hauled him up with the help of his companions.

As he was made of iron he was not choked, but hanging up he could do nothing except make grimaces like a jack-in-the-box, which was just what he looked like hanging in the air.

"Let me down!" shouted the unhappy man, "and you may draw whatever you like."

"That won't do, my friend," answered Perico, laughing at the doll's movements. "I should not be so stupid as to let you escape."

So that, as the song says:

> "Here, sirs, came to an end
> The life of Don Crispin."

"Do you think I have forgotten the punch you gave me?"

The other boys tied the rope to a sofa so as not to get tired, and led by Perico began to explore the rooms of the cave. They were all beautiful save that the ornaments on the walls were of dolls as grotesque as the master.

The way out of the grotto could not be seen anywhere. And the reason was simple, as the means of exit was by the lamp to which the doll was hanging; but the boys did not like the idea of going down one by one, with a great risk of breaking their heads.

Perico, now uneasy, recommenced to run about the rooms, and troubled by seeing on the walls what recalled his unfortunate adventure, pulled out his handkerchief and rubbed out all the drawings, seeing, with extraordinary surprise, that the boys recovered their original shapes. On rubbing out the last drawing a formidable noise was heard: the iron man vanished as if he were smoke, the palace disappeared, and they found themselves at the entrance to the cave. From there they marched to the town, where their parents were anxiously waiting for them, and there they related what had occurred.

All returned thanks to God and promised not to draw dolls again anywhere.

Perico became a very honorable man, devoted himself to drawing, and became a great artist, but he never forgot those dolls, which might have cost him so dear.

THE MAN WITH THE NOSE

The King of Persia, Abe-lan-fui, was sitting one day with his august feet in a basin of rose-water, an ingenious method which he employed in order to cause happy ideas to occur to him when he was troubled. Half slumbering by reason of the sublime thoughts which crowded to his brain, he nodded two or three times, rubbed his eyes, and reclining his head on a cushion, fell asleep. The court with silent respect contemplated the gentle sleep of his majesty, when a loud sneeze filled the courtiers with horror and suddenly awakened his majesty.

"Who was it?" asked the monarch.

"Sire!" exclaimed a youth, "it was I. I could not help it."

"Shall I hang him?" asked the Grand Vizier[11].

"Not yet; wait. You have just interrupted the sweetest dream of my life. I was just thinking how to marry Princess Chan-ta-lan to a prince of her rank when your tempestuous sneeze caused it all to go out of my head. Your duty now is to guess my dream. If you can remind me of it, I forgive you; but if not, I will have your nose shortened so that you will never sneeze again as long as you live."

"Sire!" answered the unhappy courtier, seizing his nose as if to bid it a last farewell, "my nose and my person belong to your majesty, but no doubt, if you grant me five minutes' reflection, with the help of God I will make you remember your dream."

When the brief respite granted by the king had expired, the courtier daringly approached the steps of the throne and spoke as follows:

"Mighty monarch! here is the only dream worthy of your

---

11 The Grand Vizier is one of the highest ranking heads of state.

illustrious talent. You dreamed that twelve princes solicited the white hand of the august Princess Chan-ta-lan; that eleven of them were graceful, but one had a defect; the former were powerful, and the latter of meagre fortune; however, your majesty chose the defective candidate as hereditary prince."

"If you tell me why I chose him," interrupted the monarch, "the nose is yours."

"You chose him, your majesty, for his surpassing genius, and for having vanquished his rivals in tests to which your majesty submitted them."

"Excellent. Now I remember it perfectly. May God preserve your nose for centuries and centuries, and my treasurer shall give you a thousand pieces of gold as a reward for your extraordinary understanding."

The court greeted this act of the monarch with a murmur of approval, and, at once, all those who a few minutes before fled from the young courtier as from a plague approached and felicitated him.

"Well, then," exclaimed the monarch, "I wish to follow the inspirations of the dream, whose description you have heard. From now on, the competition for aspirants to the hand of Chan-ta-lan is open. Proclaim it, Grand Vizier, to all my ambassadors, and let all courts know what my decision is. A necessary condition for the princes who aspire to be my successor is to send their portraits without delay.

"And now," he added, addressing the minstrels of the palace, "I permit you to sing my praises; and you," he said, facing his courtiers, "I tolerate to applaud me for the great talent that God has given me."

"Bravo! Bravo!" exclaimed the courtiers all together.

"You are half-hearted!" said the king. "Applaud with

more enthusiasm, then I promise you not to get angry even when you shock my modesty."

"Hurrah! Splendid! Wonderful!" cried the people of the court, applauding as if they were the claque of a theatre. "What genius! What penetration! What a pity if it should fail us!"

"Don't be afraid, it will continue to be your pride and the rejoicing of this land of fools and brutes."

"Oh, what a good lord! What a delicate compliment!"

The ambassadors announced the wish of their lord in all the capitals of the neighboring kingdoms, and very soon letters and portraits of princes in all imaginable attitudes began to arrive. Some were twirling their moustaches with a martial air; others scratched their chins as if they were irritated; and others with one hand on the hilt of their swords but wearing a magnanimous air, as if they would spare everybody's life. So the King of Persia gathered a varied collection. But amongst them one excelled for his awful simplicity, that of the Prince of Tokay[12], who appeared in full profile, showing such a deformed nose as had never been seen, not only in that town, but if you searched for ten leagues around you would not find another to approach it. And saying it is different from seeing it. For that immense, colossal nose measured from the base to the tip nearly a yard in the measure of that country, which is equal to two in Castilian measure. It was as thick as it was large, which almost caused the other features of the countenance to disappear. The painter, who undoubtedly was very clever, had expressed the air of weariness which that badly balanced weight produced in the prince, and which cried aloud for a counter weight at the back of his head.

The king laughed very much to see this phenomenon,

12   Tokaj is a region in present-day Hungary.

and on seeing him laugh the courtiers also dared to laugh at the prince; but the princess, called to see the portrait of that aspirant to marriage, far from laughing, commenced to cry disconsolately and nearly fainted.

"I do not wish to see the man with the nose!" she cried. "What great folly! With this face he dares to ask for my hand! Papa, declare war against him, take him prisoner, and do him the favor of trimming his nose, if only to oblige me!"

The court also laughed at the remarks of the princess; for to some people there is nothing more amusing than to laugh at others.

The king did not dare to disregard the Prince of Tokay, and, moreover, greatly wished to see closely that elephant's trunk; so it was that he authorised his ambassador to invite him to come to Persia to the place arranged for the other aspirants.

All Teheran[13] was burning with desire to know the princes, and especially the big-nosed one: and so on the day of his arrival all the town crowded to the gate by which he was to enter the capital. The Prince of Tokay, accompanied by his inseparable nose and a modest escort, entered the city and proceeded directly to the palace.

"What beauty!" cried the people. "With such a nose, well distributed, there would be an end to all the pug-nosed people in the world."

The king, who came out to receive him, wished to embrace him as etiquette required, but knocked against his nose and nearly tore out his eye. At last a courtier held carefully aside the nose and he was able to accomplish the palatine ceremony.

13   Tehran was, and remains, the capital of Persia.

"His nose is tremendous," said the king, putting wet cloths on his injured eye; "but it does not seem to me so large as the one in the portrait."

"I am of the same opinion," added the princess. "It seems to me three or four inches shorter than that the painter represented. If an artist here had done the same to me as he did to the Prince of Tokay I am sure that I should order him to receive a sound thrashing!"

"Then, to blow his nose how many handkerchiefs are wanted!" said a courtier.

"He blows his nose on a sheet," added another.

The following day all the princes were summoned to give proof of their talents. All went about very thoughtfully except he of Tokay, who arrived with a most natural and quiet demeanor.

"My lord princes," said the sovereign, taking his seat on the throne, "in order to decide who is the son-in-law who suits me best I have arranged to put your knowledge to a test, now that your personal charms are to be seen."

All the spectators looked at the big-nosed prince, who seemed as tranquil as if he were not the object of general curiosity.

"Here are the questions that you have to answer. Which is the most valuable thing in the world? How many baskets full of earth could be taken from the mountain which is to be seen from the palace? And who is the most treacherous companion that we all have?"

He granted them an hour in which to think out the answers, each being shut up separately. He formed a tribunal composed of the wisest men of his kingdom, and afterwards compared the aspirants to his daughter's hand one with the other.

Some stated that these questions were too difficult for such rapid answers; others said what they thought about them in such a stupid way that the tribunal and the court could not refrain from laughter.

At length it came to the turn of the Prince of Tokay, who, bowing respectfully, answered, "The most valuable thing in the world is life, because it is God's most wonderful work. The mountain which is to be seen from the palace has exactly two baskets full of earth, provided a basket is made large enough to hold half the mountain. And the most treacherous companion is time, which is our friend in youth, our companion in middle age, and finally kills us treacherously in old age."

The king smiled, the tribunal approved, and the court applauded. The princess herself appeared enchanted.

"Without any doubt," said the monarch, "you are the the victor in this contest of intelligence; now it remains for you to vanquish in strength and skill."

A stand was erected in the public place for the king, the judges, and the court, and shortly afterwards the princes, bearing their arms and mounted on superb horses, rode into the lists.

Each one was given a lance and the struggle began. The first of the princes fought with the second, the conqueror with the third, and so on.

The Prince of Muscovy[14], who was a robust man, won the greater part of the contest, wounding his adversaries seriously by lance-thrusts, throwing them from their horses, and making them declare themselves vanquished under the threat of <u>finishing them off</u> like lambs. When the last one appeared, the

14   Muscovy refers to Moscow, and the Prince of Muscovy refers to the Prince of the Grand Duchy of Moscow.

feeble Prince of Tokay, a murmur of pity went round the spectators. He of Muscovy had nothing even to start on! Moreover, as that nose could not be covered by any known helmet, the prince kept it outside with his visor raised. This was a manifest disadvantage, for the other was cased in armor from top to toe.

He of Muscovy approached the stand where the princess was and said to her:

"Beautiful Chan-ta-lan, I know that you have a whim to have the Prince of Tokay's nose shortened, and I intend to pull it out by the roots and offer it to you as a wedding gift."

And saying this, he attacked his adversary, who was quietly awaiting him. Their lances struck against their shields and broke into splinters; the horses reared, but neither one nor the other moved from the saddle. The lances being broken, they seized their swords and struck at each other furiously until the blades were broken also. The Prince of Tokay approached his adversary, and with only one hand—incredible strength!—took him from the saddle and threw him rolling on the ground.

Tremendous applause followed, and the Prince of Tokay was cheered on all sides. The latter alighted from his horse, and drawing near to his enemy, who was not yet able to rise, made him admit his defeat. The princess looked at him in amazement and confusion, and the king said to her: "So you have got to have the big-nosed one! However, console yourself, we will give him a case for it."

The prince approached the stand, and after receiving the king's congratulations, the princess said to him:

"I confess, Prince of Tokay, that you are not handsome, that you lack something, or rather that you have something too much, but such proofs have you given of your ingenuity and strength that I will be your wife without feeling any repugnance."

"My beautiful princess," exclaimed the knight, "I am so grateful for your kindness that I do not wish to embitter your happiness without making you a present which I think will be very much to your taste. My adversary offered to give you my nose, the cause of your past antipathy, and now that he has not succeeded in his project, may I be permitted to present it to you myself."

So saying, to the great surprise of every one, he gave a sharp tug at his nose, tearing it off at one stroke. The crowd gave a shout, believing that the man was going to die, when to the general astonishment it was seen that under that cardboard nose he wore his own natural nose, which was so delicate and well proportioned that he had no need to envy even the best shaped of noses. The Prince of Tokay was none other than the courtier of the sneeze.

"I appealed to this expedient," he said, "because I wished you to know and love me only for my qualities, and not for my face, for beauty passes away quickly, and talent is a divine gift and much more lasting."

The princess nearly died of joy on seeing her sweetheart so clever, and the rare event formed the conversation of all the city.

The wedding was celebrated with great pomp, and the new couple were very happy, according to what the chronicles of Persia say.

In one of the princess's rooms, under a pretty lantern, was the cardboard nose of the false Prince of Tokay. Under it was the following inscription: "Physical defects count as noth-

ing when the heart is generous and noble and the understanding clear."

THE ISLAND OF BRILLIANTS

The bark *Esperanza* with all canvas spread was sailing the China Sea, when a violent storm overtook her. The event was so rapid that it gave no time to be foreseen, and the captain, who was an old sea-dog, as sailors are called who have become inured to dangers, did not foresee that the breeze of an instant ago would change so soon into a violent hurricane. The rudder was broken by the force of the waves, and the ship was driven by the cyclone without means of defence—the crew and the bark were lost.

All believed their last moment had come, since without doubt the boat would go to pieces on the rocks which could be seen at a short distance, when the captain gave a shout which calmed the anxiety of all hearts.

"The Island of Brilliants!" he exclaimed, and instantly all appeared in order to contemplate it.

"Good," said a sailor. "That may be the Island of Brilliants, but if striking against it breaks my head, I don't care whether it is against a stone worth twopence or against a diamond worth ten millions."

"You are right," answered the captain, "but the storm has abated a little, and it remains for us to launch the boats and approach the coast in them."

This was done. A few minutes afterwards all the sailors save one embarked in the boats and went to the island, which was visible not far off.

In the bark there remained an Aragonese[15] passenger called Antonio, who had set his heart on getting to Manila[16],

15   Aragon is an autonomous region in present-day northeastern Spain, between Madrid and Barcelona.

16   Manila is the present-day capital of the Philippines.

and who said he would continue on the ship even if he arrived alone at the capital of the Magallanico archipelago.

"But," said they to him, "don't be mad. Don't you see that you will certainly perish?"

"That we shall see; for I am going to Manila even if I have to swim there."

And there was no means of convincing him; therefore they left him to his fate. The boats separated from the ship and went off to the Island of Brilliants.

The captain, meanwhile, said to his shipwrecked companions:

"The island is inhabited by ill-tempered dwarfs who kill those who cause them inconvenience, and, on the other hand, to those who appear amiable they grant whatever they are asked. So, gentlemen, I recommend moderation."

This they promised him, and in a little while the boats touched dry land.

They disembarked, running the boats aground so that the surf should not break them up, and penetrated into the island.

They had gone scarcely a mile when they saw some little white houses of brick, white as snow, and of a singular shape. They looked like jars turned upside down. All the houses had very small windows and a small door.

"This must be," said the captain, "the dwarfs' city. Be very careful now, because this is a dangerous moment."

"But where are the brilliants?" asked a sailor.

"They are on that mountain which begins at the side of the town. It is quite inaccessible except by a narrow path whose entrance is carefully and strongly defended by the dwarfs."

At this moment a kind of bugle sounded and an arrow appeared from each little window. They had given the alarm and the dwarfs hastened to the defence.

The captain tied a handkerchief to the end of a stick, and with this improvised flag made signals that his intentions were pacific.

Then a committee of dwarfs came out to talk matters over with them, making themselves understood by signs, and at last agreed to let the shipwrecked men enter the town, but blindfolded.

They submitted to this condition, and immediately were surrounded by a good number of guards, who manacled them and presently imprisoned them in some very small cells, so small that the newcomers were obliged to cower down almost all day because they touched the roof with their heads.

On the following day they were taken into the presence of the chief of the dwarfs, who was the youngest of all, but who must have been the most learned, because, after having asked them in several languages what their nationality was, spoke to them in Spanish as follows:

"What brought you to this island? Do you not know that he who comes to it never returns? Perhaps the desire for wealth has moved you? If so, you were much mistaken, because the riches which exist here are for us. So that now you know what your fate must be—either to die or to be our slaves."

And at this a crowd of dwarfs approached the surprised sailors, and without giving them time to defend themselves, tied them up and led them back again to their prisons.

All this while the bark *Esperanza* was going along abandoned to the mercy of the elements, and our Aragonese, fear-ing nothing, sat tranquilly in the bows, saying to the ship:

"I must go to Manila; so now you know what to do."

The wind and the waves were driving the ship forward, until one morning, the tempest now being over, Antonio found himself in a sort of natural harbor where the ship ran on to the sand.

"Well, this must be Manila!" he exclaimed, and throwing himself over the side into the water, he reached dry land in two strides, not without having previously taken, as a measure of precaution, a revolver, a gun, a cutlass, and a pouch full of cartridges.

"They won't throw me out of Manila for want of arms!" he said, and going on and on, our good Antonio with his gun on his shoulder commenced to look for people to ask the way to the capital of the archipelago, now lost to the Spaniards.

After several hours' walk he met two dwarfs who, seated on the ground, were playing marbles with some stones whose brilliance was dazzling.

The Aragonese approached the players and bade them good afternoon; the dwarfs raised their heads and looked at him contemptuously and continued to play.

"Look here, I said 'Good afternoon' to you," shouted the Aragonese, "and in my country when an insult is offered one knows what happens."

The dwarfs turned to look at him without having understood, and then Antonio, with two superb punches, knocked the presumptuous dwarfs to the ground. One remained stunned and could not move himself; but the other began to run away, uttering cries, and disappeared.

The Aragonese brought round the dwarf and detained him.

For several days they went about the mountain, and during this time Antonio succeeded in learning a few phrases of the strange language which the dwarf spoke, and the latter learned several others in Spanish, with which they came to understand each other perfectly. The two friends related their respective histories to one another. That of the dwarf was short; he was called Fu-fei, and he was a captain of the Cuirassiers of the Guard; and as they had no real horses they rode some made of cane so prettily that they attracted attention. He narrated, moreover, that some days before, some giants who had arrived then were made prisoners, and were to be killed or made slaves. As soon as he gave these details of the prisoners Antonio cried, "These are my people. I will not go to Manila until they are out of trouble."

"While you are here," said Fu-fei, "don't run any risks; because my companions never go up the mountains, as it makes them tired, and they are under the care of the doctor who prevents them from tiring themselves; but if you go down to the plain they will attack you, and they are more than three thousand."

"I don't care; I shall know how to defend myself."

"Then let me recommend you to do one thing. When you begin to fight I will signal to you which is the company of archers who use poisoned arrows. Shoot at them, and you can laugh at the rest."

And so it was. At the moment when he went down the mountain, Antonio found himself attacked by the outposts of the dwarfs' army. Fu-fei pointed out the company of the terrible arrows, and the Aragonese destroyed it by shots from his gun and blows with his cutlass.

"There is our king!" cried Fu-fei, pointing to a little dwarf who was scarcely sixteen inches in height.

"Then I will talk things over with your king immediately."

And, gently taking hold of him by the neck so as not to hurt him, he put the king in his pocket. Arriving at an oak-tree which would be about two yards high, and sitting down in the shade, he took the king out of his pocket and said:

"Where are the prisoners? Either give them back to me or this is the moment when you lose your position, your crown, and your life."

The dwarf king answered in Spanish that he would give the prisoners up and whatever they might wish in exchange for his liberty! And so our hero with his two dwarfs under his arm walked on to Dwarftown, as the town was called. Once inside he put the king on the ground in order to recover all his dignity, and the monarch ordered the Spanish prisoners to be set free.

When the latter recognised their liberator, they did not know what to do to show their gratitude.

"Don't you know how?" asked Antonio. "Well, take me to Manila, for I am in a hurry."

"But," answered the captain, "would you go away from this island without carrying off any diamonds?"

"Where are they?" asked the Aragonese.

"There, on the top of that mountain," they said to him.

"Good gracious! Just now I was in the midst of them and didn't notice. The truth is," he added, "that what I wanted was something to eat, and for half a pound of roasted meat I would have given all the diamonds of the earth."

Finally they all went to the mountain, gathered the diamonds in handfuls, and when they could carry no more, they went back towards the spot where the bark was ashore, and there after several months' work they succeeded in fixing a new rudder and some masts, which although small were sufficient to make the boat go. They put out to sea and at last arrived at Manila, to the great satisfaction of the Aragonese, who exclaimed:

"Did I not tell you that the ship would bring me to Manila?"

The dwarf Fu-fei had not wished to part with his friend and accompanied him everywhere, exciting attention by his long beard and tiny stature. The poor fellow was obliged to go about the streets singing, so that people should avoid treading on him.

They all soon returned to Spain, where they sold their diamonds and bought fine farms, founding an agricultural colony, in which they all lived together like brothers.

THE JUDGMENT OF THE FLOWERS

"Is it true that the rose is the queen of the flowers?" asked Richard of his papa.

And the latter said to him jokingly:

"Ask them themselves, they ought to be better informed."

Richard took what his father told him literally, and going down into the garden, approached a plum-tree which gallantly waved to and fro in the wind, and taking off his hat with great respect, asked it:

"Mr. Plum-tree, will you be good enough to tell me if the rose is the queen of the flowers?"

But the plum-tree continued to move to and fro in the wind without answering him.

And drawing near to an almond tree, whose white blossoms had just opened, he repeated his question.

"Mr. Almond-tree, is it true that the rose is the queen of the flowers?"

The almond-tree remained silent, but its blossoms went red with envy.

"The almond-tree is also unprincipled," thought Richard. "All these trees have a discourteous tone. Let us ask the plants."

A splendid double pink, which raised its splendid corolla with a gallantry worthy of its nobility, as soon as he heard the question, graciously bowed upon his stalk and answered:

"Quite so, the rose is our beloved queen, on account of being so beautiful and because her delicate aroma has no rival. But if you wish to know more, come back to-night at twelve o'clock and notice what happens in your garden."

"Thank you, kind pink. I will not miss to-night."

Richard went to bed at the usual time, but he could not sleep. At half-past eleven he dressed himself again, and slipping secretly down stairs arrived in the garden and awaited events. On the last stroke of midnight a bright light appeared from the sky and that ray of light condensed on the earth, taking the figure of a beautiful woman crowned with flowers, who carried in her hand a little golden wand which gave off brilliant reflections. The fairy extended her hand and immediately an unusual movement was produced among the plants. The pinks turned into elegant gentlemen in bright costumes of ruby, pink, and green; the hyacinths and jasmines into gallant little pages with fair hair; the white lilies were pale ladies of singular beauty, dressed in white; the dahlias wore long trains and at the neck a ruffle of delicate lace of colors which recalled the flowers which had preceded; the violet modestly tried to hide her beautiful countenance of velvety skin and her eyes of gentle aspect among a group of poppies, who passed arm-in-arm, attracting attention by their blood red costumes. Finally from amongst a group of mornful evergreens, who were chatting with some beautiful pansies, appeared the queen of the fête, the rose. Her presence produced a murmur of admiration, never had she been so lovely. Her face held the freshness of the flower, and her pink dress with a long train was of very fine silk which rustled as the sovereign walked. An olive-tree turned into a throne and dais, and the rose, without any other ceremony than a general greeting, took her seat on the throne. She raised her arm, imposing silence, and everybody became silent.

"Gentlemen," said the queen, "once again the good magician Spring has re-animated our hearts. We have not met since last year and there are several grave matters to resolve, but the most important is the manner of defending ourselves from the bees, wasps, and butterflies who continually sip our honey, accelerating our end. On this point I have already begged Spring to have the accused appear before me, so that this gathering is really an oral judgment."

At a signal from the magician the accused appeared in costumes of etiquette, the butterfly wearing its finest clothes.

It appeared before the queen with its head modestly bent and its face lighted up by a blush.

"What does your majesty wish?" it asked.

"To inquire the motive why you presume to take away our nectar," said the rose.

"Ah, madam!" replied the butterfly, touched, "little harm I do you, because I never take more than is necessary to feed myself, and I have never abused your hospitality."

"That is well; we will take that into account as an extenuating circumstance for you. Let the wasp approach."

The wasp entered in a black dress-coat and a yellow necktie striped with black.

"I," it said, "gather nectar from you because I have proposed to work like the bee, although I have not yet succeeded in doing so since the beginning of the world, but still not much time has passed and I hope to learn."

"How can you hope to learn," interrupted the queen, "if all that you do is to eat it all without having any to make honeycombs? Your case is a very bad one. As you have not a good lawyer you are lost. Fetch the bee."

The latter appeared, her presence awakening a general murmur. It wore neither a dress-coat nor a frock-coat, nor even a lounge-coat; it was wearing a blouse covered with stains of honey and wax. All drew away from the bee for fear of getting soiled.

"Now I know what I am coming to," it said without keeping quiet. "It is always the same song: that we do take away, that we do not take away the nectar from the flowers. Good, what about it? We do not do so for ourselves, but for our master. All the sweet syrup of your corollas we enclose in the hive, and from there every year it comes out so that Man, our master, rejoices his palate with it and embalms his breath with your aroma. After dying in summer and losing your green leaves in autumn, you still live in us, that we may make your remembrance lasting. And still you complain! You, it is true, give your blood, but it would be worth nothing if we did not gather it in order to store it. The work is ours, and the work is worth as much as your nectar. If you have to condemn me, do so quickly, I beg of you, as I am losing a great deal of work time, and we are somewhat behindhand with the work."

The rose called the pink and the violet, discussed the case with them, and after some minutes' reflection, spoke in this manner:

"The wasp is an unconscientious glutton who, under the pretext of making honeycombs, which she never succeeds in doing, robs us. Give her five hundred hard lashes."

On hearing this a deadly nightshade seized the wasp and carried her away to bestow the correction.

"The butterfly's innocence and moderation favor her," said the queen, "therefore I declare her absolved with all favorable pronouncements."

The butterfly bowed respectfully and kissed the sovereign's hand. Her golden feelers glistened, she shook her wings, filling the ambient air with diamond dust, and took to flight showering cascades of light.

"With regard to the bee," continued the rose, "not only do I find her without any guilt, but wish that henceforth you do not close your petals to her, but leave her at liberty to carry away the honey that she requires. As a reward for her laboriousness, and as a symbol of perpetual friendship between us, I am going to give her a kiss."

The bee, much moved, advanced, and placing her blushing forehead within reach of the queen's lips, received a kiss of peace, which made tears of gratitude gather in her eyes.

A delicious perfume invaded the garden, the fairy raised her wand, and each flower returned to its post, recovering its original form.

The magician flew into space, wrapped in a moonbeam, and Richard remained alone, pensive in the recollection of what he had seen.

"What a beautiful lesson!" he said. "Even in the kingdom of flowers work gains the most precious reward."

THE THREE QUESTIONS

In the history of Spain, King Pedro I of Castile[17], son of Alfonso XI the *Just*, is known by the surname of the *Cruel*.

And his fame as a heartless man was such that his subjects, on whom he satisfied his terrible thirst for blood and violence, held him in great terror.

One day while hunting, of which sport he was very fond, King Pedro lost his way in the wood, and came to rest himself—the night being well advanced—in an hospitable convent, where without being known he was offered food, bed, and shelter.

Hardly returning thanks, he passed into the refectory, and on entering was recognised by a lay brother, who knew that the king suffered from a certain illness called arthritis, the principal effect of which was that the malady produced, when he was walking, a strange sound of bones knocking together.

By this noise he was recognised by the lay brother.

Instantly informing the community, due homage was hastily rendered to the monarch; but King Pedro was in a bad temper, and facing one of the reverend fathers, said to him in a disconcerting tone:

"How fat you are, Father Prior! Study makes no hollows in you, from which I gather that you cannot be so wise as the people hereabout say."

The community was so taken aback, that no one dared to say a word to that monster of a king.

"Well, if you wish to please me," he continued, "I sum-

---

17   Castile was a region and kingdom in present-day central-northern Spain.

mon you to come to my palace within ten days, and to answer satisfactorily the following questions: First, what is the distance between the earth and the sun? Second, how much am I worth? And third, what do I believe which is false? If you do not answer me to my taste I will have you beheaded at once."

And saying this, he went away.

Needless to say the poor friar was frightened, for he knew only too well that King Pedro was quite capable of doing what he threatened.

And he devoted himself to thinking day and night about the questions, without hitting upon any answers.

At the time when King Pedro reigned the distance between the planets had not been discovered, so there were many discussions between the brethren over the questions of the king. They were still disputing when the day arrived on which the prior was summoned to the palace. And even yet he did not know what to answer. In his distress he invoked the Holy Virgin, certain that She would not refuse to help him.

After which he was about to set out for Seville when one of the lay brothers, a sharp and daring lad, said to him:

"Father Prior, your reverence and I are about the same height, and even look somewhat alike. Why not let me go in your place, father, and answer the king?"

On seeing him so resolved he did not doubt for a moment that the lay brother had been inspired by God to save him, and after hearing him, allowed him to go to Seville.

At the moment in which he arrived at the palace and announced himself, the king gave orders for him to be allowed to enter.

"Have you thought out the answers to the questions that I asked you?" asked King Pedro.

"Yes, sire."

"Well, begin then. What is the distance between the earth and the sun?"

"Eight hundred and forty-seven thousand leagues. Not one more, nor one less. And if your majesty does not believe me, have it measured."

As this was impossible, the king was obliged to say that he was satisfied.

"Not bad," he said. "Now the second: How much am I worth?"

"Twenty-nine pieces of silver."

"And why twenty-nine pieces?"

"Because your majesty is not worth so much as our Savior, Jesus Christ, and He was sold for thirty."

"And what do I think which is not true?" exclaimed King Pedro, somewhat piqued.

"Well, your majesty thinks that I am the prior, and I am not."

The king was surprised at the ingenuity of the lay brother and pardoned the substitution, and heaped both with favors.

This proves that the fiercest men are overcome and appeased by the forces of ingenuity.

THE CAPTAIN'S EXPLOIT

"What ruins are those which are to be seen on the top of that ridge?" asked a genteel captain of the policeman of a village.

"The accursed ruins!" answered the first authority of the village with extreme terror. "Many years ago," he said, "there used to be a fine castle there, inhabited by a feudal lord who was more avaricious than anybody in the world before. There stands his statue amidst the rubbish, and terrible stories are told about it which frighten all the neighbors.

"In the archives of the town several curious documents are kept, and if your worship, Sir Captain, wishes to read them, I will lend them to you with great pleasure."

The soldier smiled disdainfully on hearing the policeman, and begged him to let him see those curious documents, because he had the idea of visiting the ruins and removing for ever the superstitious fear that they inspired.

That night he received a bundle of yellowed papers falling to pieces through age and dampness, and shut up in his room he read them from beginning to end.

The following morning when Captain Pero Gil—for such was his name—went out into the square, the hollows of a night of insomnia and fever were clearly seen in his face. What had happened to him?

Among the papers which formed the bundle, one above all had attracted his attention. It ran more or less as follows:

"It is said by neighbor Nuno Perez that in the castle, at the foot of the tower of Homage, there must be an immense treasure, but it is guarded by one hundred dwarfs with long beards who strike anybody who comes near.

"At twelve o'clock in the night a gap opens in the ground

which gives access to enormous riches piled up in the cellar; but exactly at one o'clock the earth closes up until the following night. If, instead of one person, two or three go to the place, then the earth does not open and the treasure remains hidden.

"That is the news which, on the evidence of an eyewitness, has reached me, and which I certify.—Inigo Lopez, the constable."

The captain remained perplexed for a good while, and at last said to himself resolutely: "Tomorrow night I will go to the tower of Homage at the foot of the castle."

Indeed, at twelve o'clock in the night he went out of the house where he lodged and went towards the ruins, first making sure that his sword came out of the sheath without difficulty, and that the pistols which he wore in his belt were well loaded.

At eleven o'clock, or a little later, he arrived at the castle. A splendid moon was shining, which gave the landscape a melancholy appearance. The captain hid himself behind some stones close to the big tower, and there waited, twisting his moustache, to see the marvel take place. The village clock struck twelve, and on the last stroke the earth opened and a crowd of dwarfs, with beards down to the ground, came out of the narrow gap. They were armed with thick sticks, and began to dance round the entrance of the vault, singing:

> *"Let us defend the treasure,*
> *Let us defend our gold*
> *Against every mortal*
> *Not knowing the signal."*

The captain advanced quickly, and taking up his place at the side of the circle of little men, saluted the dwarfs with great courtesy.

"Good evening, friends,"

"Daring man!" said the tiny men. "Who are you? What have you come here for?"

And armed with their thick sticks they rushed towards the intruder. But the latter, without being frightened, unsheathed his sword, and said to them very calmly:

"Let us be serious, comrades, and leave off making bad-natured jokes, because I will cut down any one who comes too near me. Are you willing to let me have the treasures?"

"Never!" they exclaimed. "It is necessary for you to give us the signal. If you do not know it, we shall kill you."

"That is easier said than done," said Pero Gil, with great deliberation. "You must grow a little before you can put a man like me in pickle. If your height had grown as much as your beard, it might have been different."

"Let us kill him," shouted the dwarfs. "He does not know the signal!"

And they threw themselves upon the captain. But the latter drew out a pistol, and with one shot the most daring of them fell to the ground, which checked the rest.

"It seems that I came off best," said the captain, laughing. "What I have done to this fellow I will do to the remainder if you come near. Therefore let me pass without hindrance."

"We would let ourselves be killed before permitting you to get to the treasure, unless you gave us the signal."

"And what signal is that?"

"We cannot tell you."

"It seems to me that I shall not require it for grinding up

your ribs."

"Away! Away!" said the little men; and armed with their sticks they rushed upon Pero Gil. The latter fired off his second pistol, bowling over another, but they threw themselves upon him, until his back looked like a snake turning round amidst the crowd of those who were attacking him. At last he saw that he was surrounded and defenceless, and therefore was obliged to jump over the wall at the risk of being dashed to pieces, and so left the place, ashamed of his defeat.

"My goodness! what can the signal be?" he asked himself while on his way to the village.

The following morning he returned to the ruins, armed with a lever, and recognised the place where on the previous night he had seen the opening. There was nothing there! However much he poked about he could not find the least sign which showed the entrance to the mysterious vault; and what was still stranger, he could not distinguish the slightest trace of the past fight.

Then he resolved to try if cunning could succeed where strength had failed.

The following night he hid himself in the ruins and watched the place where the marvellous event took place. The dwarfs came out with their accustomed dance and song:

> "Let us defend the treasure,
> Let us defend our gold
> Against every mortal
> Not knowing the signal."

The dance over, one of them said:

"The captain will not return, but if he does come back we

will kill him."

"It would be better to allow him to enter the vault and there let him die of hunger."

"And if he seizes the bell?"

"Then we are lost."

"But he must first give the statue of the old master of the castle a thrust with his sword."

Pero Gil did not wait to hear any more, and at one bound approached the statue, which was situated in what used to be the armory of the fortress, and struck it a stout blow with his blade.

The statue fell down flat as if struck by lightning, and at once the dwarfs surrounded the captain and forced him down a flight of steps.

Hardly had he entered than the gap closed up and the captain found himself alone in a cave which was lighted by a lamp hanging from the ceiling. On the floor there were great heaps of gold and precious stones, but this was not the thing that claimed the captain's attention. He was looking for the bell which he had heard the dwarfs speak about.

For half an hour his search was fruitless. He turned over the yellow piles of money and the sacks of gems, but the desired object was not to be found.

Weary and perspiring he threw himself down on a pile of gold bars, and there rested before again returning to his task.

The mysterious bell had to be found.

Persuaded that it was not to be come across in a visible spot, he began to strike the walls, until at last one of them sounded hollow. With his sword he made a hole and from it drew out a leaden bell of a very rare shape, which in a good sale might be worth as much as four farthings.

"And now what must I do?" thought the captain. He carefully examined the object he had found, which bore the following inscription, "Do not ring me unless you know how." But the captain was not a man to hesitate, and rang the bell. Immediately the walls closed together, threatening to crush him by their enormous mass. Without being daunted he gave another ring, and then a thousand points of steel came forth from the walls as if they were going to pass through him. Then he gave a third ring, and immediately the vault returned to its original form.

At the fourth the dwarfs humbly presented themselves and said to him:

"What do you want of us? Command us as your slaves."

"In the first place, to dance the saraband[18] in order to amuse me, as a compensation for the unpleasant time you have given me."

And the dwarfs danced like anything for a good while, until Pero Gil told them to stop.

"Now you will take the sacks of money and carry them to my house."

The dwarfs obeyed without making the slightest observation, loading up those precious things.

"Leave us the bell," they said, "since you take away the riches."

Pero Gil was going to leave it, when he suddenly had a presentiment and thought better of it.

"This talisman shall never leave me."

Then the dwarfs carried the riches to his house, singing on the way:

---

18   The saraband is a slow Spanish dance.

"Don't let us guard the treasure now,
For it is being taken away
By this fortunate mortal
Who knows the signal."

So Captain Pero Gil became master of immense riches, which he distributed among his soldiers, naturally keeping for himself the largest part.

And whenever he thought of that famous adventure, he rightly used to say, "After all, the true talisman to get what we want is cunning and bravery."

THE TOPSY-TURVY WORLD

I don't know why, but it is a fact that Providence one day decreed that everything should turn upside down. The picture that the world presented could not have been more extraordinary: the fishes flew through the air like swarms of butterflies; in place of linnets and nightingales, the sharks and whales sang. The birds swam on the bosom of the waters, like Pedro for his house; it was glorious to see the dives they made. A donkey in the porch of an Inn played on a clarinet the "No me matas, no me matas," while another who was apparently in a good position, came out of a restaurant picking his teeth with a Toledo sword.

It is related that a boy who lived at that time, and whose name was, if I remember right, Manolo, had, among other grave defects, that of ill-treating animals; his parents and masters reprimanded him in vain, and from time to time even gave him a flogging that would have set fire to tinder: but it did not make the boy any better. Whenever he saw an ass tied to a fence he untied it and rode it for a good while, hitting it a whack to make it trot. When he met a dog the least that he did was to fetch it a smack that made it go away at more than a walking pace with its tail between its legs. More than one cat he chased about after having tied a sardine tin to its tail; in short, he was a little demon.

But now it must be remembered that all things were changed, and that on waking up one morning he found, at the head of his bed, one of his dogs, which, giving him a punch, said:

"Little friend, on getting up you have got to clean my boots;" and as the boy hesitated, the dog hit him two punches which made him get up more than quickly. What was his surprise to notice that he could only go on four feet! He wished to speak, but a bark came from his lips; he tried to bite the dog, and the latter rained blows upon him.

He rushed out of the house, and found other boys as mischievous as himself punished in the same way. In Oriente Place, Carlos and Pepe were pulling a little carriage, and in it were riding the two goats that usually drew the vehicle. Several of those water-carriers who carry their water-skins on the loins of a donkey which they almost kill by blows, went about themselves bent down under the load, getting a blow each time they sucked their thumbs. Their former slaves went on two feet behind them, saying: "Gee up, donkey, you are more stupid than a post."

Manolo went on his way, on four feet of course, and even these seemed few enough to run with, when on crossing a street he met a friend and schoolmate, with whom he opened, by barks, the following dialogue:

"Bernardo, as I live! Have you seen what has happened to us?"

"Yes, of course I see it! For am I not changed into a poodle?"

"Here you see me in a fix; I don't know where to hide myself so that the old dogs won't be able to take their revenge for the tricks I used to play on them when I was a person."

At this moment a noise was heard, and on turning round they saw a tramcar drawn by some of those drovers who are always complaining, and on the platform was a mule coquettishly adorned with a cocked hat, driving the car, which was full of all kinds of animals.

"My boy," said Manolo to Bernardo, "do you know that

instead of a tramcar that looks more like Noah's Ark!"

He had hardly uttered these words when he felt himself seized and secured, and his shirt was pulled out at the back, and to the tail of it was tied a petrol can. He turned his head, and then saw all the dogs gathered together which formerly he used to hurt, and who now were celebrating with great laughter the happy event of making Manolo run with the can tied to his tail. Two kicks well given rid him of all doubt and made him start running as fast as he could.

On passing close to a tank he saw some fishes which, with a rod under their fins, were angling for boys who were swimming about. At last he stopped half dead from fatigue, being taken up by an old, blind horse, which sported eye-protectors, and which, in exchange for some crusts, made him learn some exercises with which to amuse the appreciative audience of bears, monkeys, dogs, cats, and other distinguished people.

The horse, seated on the ground, with a silk hat which resembled a concertina[19], played on a little drum "The Paraguay Polka," while Manolo danced to it. So much dancing made him tired, and one day he gave the old horse the slip, leaving him alone with the drum. Naturally the loss was announced in the *Gazette*, and a reward was even offered to any one who found him, but all was useless, because the latter hid himself in order not to get caught.

One afternoon he saw many people—if we can call cats, dogs, mules, etc., people—gather together and enter a large building.

"Dear me!" said Manolo, "this is the bull-ring! All right, as a dog I can go in and see the fight free."

And slipping between two animals who acted as porters,

---

19   The concertina is a hexagon-shaped, accordion-like instrument.

he went into the ring and took a seat.

Divine Power! What a spectacle! A fat donkey, which acted as master of ceremonies, had at his side in the box another as asinine as himself, and it was the latter who told him when it was necessary to change the programme.

A number of peacocks adorned with airy mantles filled the boxes, and with opera-glasses and lorgnettes looked at each other, criticising and ridiculing each other disparagingly. How many animals there were in all parts of the ring! Round the arena barrier it was crowded with bears carrying leather bottles filled with wine, which they delicately raised. There was great confusion, until a band, or rather an orchestra, of ostriches played a gay double step, the toreadors appearing immediately after. What a fight it was! Twelve bulls from the most celebrated breeding studs came out on two feet with the red cloth airily placed between their horns. Those which acted as spearmen rode on the boys who clean up the ring, and carried very long spears. The trumpet sounded, and the first animal appeared in the arena; it was a German, who attacked the spearmen, overthrowing two boys. The master of ceremonies made a sign that it was now time to use the darts. The audience protested, shouting: "Donkey, donkey! you don't understand!" The donkey M.C. took off his hat, and the audience asked that the darts should be stuck in the toreadors. Cuernosgrandes, who was the first killer, tried to fix his pair, as badly, more or less, as the old toreadors, when a horrible shouting arose in the arena, and such formidable fighting took place that two monkeys, who had been beautiful English girls, seated at Manolo's side, fainted, and the audience rushed to the doors of the bull-ring: the German had jumped over the barrier. Manolo felt two kicks behind, and without even turning his head to see who gave them, rushed into the street like a mad animal.

Then came the worst. Some geese with Roman helmets on their heads, riding upon sardine tins, were pretending to maintain order with their sabres, and playing a number of foolish tricks upon the authorities. They soon knocked down poor little Manolo, who was obliged to seek refuge in a doorway, when a camel stopped him by laying a hand on him, saying:

"Thank goodness, I have a little dog."

The wretched camel put on a lady's veil, took Manolo in its arms as if he were a wee baby, and taking up its place in a corner, began to sing in a falsetto voice:

> *"I was born in a wood of coconut trees*
> *One morning in the month of April."*

"Gentlemen," it added, "alms for this poor mother who has a child to support." But Manolo, who did not wish to play the part of an infant in arms, gave the camel a bite in the arm and ran away to the outskirts of the town. In a cottage he found two doves, which, on seeing him so thin and hollow-cheeked, offered him their assistance and gave him something to eat. A sympathetic swallow gently looked after him, and the lullaby of its song made the poor boy sleep soundly. A feeling of sweet well-being pervaded his little body, he saw in his dreams a cloud of rose and gold, and in it the white figure of an angel which, gently moving its wings, arrived at his side and in a melodious voice said to him:

"Manuel, your sufferings have ended; let what you have seen be a warning to you, and try to be good to everybody, including animals."

The boy woke up, looked around him and found himself in his own bed, and soon the servant came in to tell him that it was now time to go to school. Manolo, who had not got over his astonishment, dressed himself quickly, noticing, full of surprise, that he went on two legs—as if he had gone all his life on four.

He never ill-treated an animal again, for this was what he said:

"Besides it being cowardly to ill-treat defenceless beings, is it not dangerous to expose oneself to the risk of the tables being turned and finding oneself in the same disagreeable position?"

DON SUERO THE PROUD

Once there was, in very remote times, a knight named Don Suero de las Navas, feudal lord of a number of Spanish villages, with a quantity of titles sufficient to fill one of the biggest pages, so many and so long were they.

Now, this knight was so proud that he thought it was a great dishonor to learn how to read and write things which he considered not only useless for a man of his accomplishments, but even shameful for a noble so rich as he was, who could indulge in the luxury of a secretary. And so it was indeed, that a poor man, who on account of his humble condition was obliged to learn those trifling necessities, went, like a vagabond, behind his master, pen and ink in satchel, ready to put into good Castilian the thousand and one mistakes that Don Suero frequently made.

On a certain occasion the king summoned the powerful Don Suero to go with his soldiers to the war, and as it could not be otherwise, the poor secretary, carrying a pen instead of a sword and a horn inkstand instead of an arrow, was obliged to place himself at the side of his lord and to march to the war.

At the beginning all went well. The orders and the letters acquainting the king with the results of the struggle were written by the hand of the unfortunate secretary, who earned each month, if my particulars are not wrong, the enormous sum of two silver threepenny pieces. Enough to have a carriage and to build good castles—in the air!

But an arrow shot at hazard in the fury of the fight against the Moors[20] put Don Lesmes, for so the secretary was called,

20   The Moors refer to the Muslim inhabitants of Iberia (corresponding largely to present-day Spain and Portugal), and Sicily and Malta in medieval times.

out of action, and Don Suero was under the necessity of seeking a new dependant who knew how to read and write—not an easy matter at that time.

He could not find one, to his great unhappiness; and if he had not had that quantity of pride in his body, he would surely have felt his lack of education, which might place him in an awkward situation, which happened soon afterwards.

He was engaged in a campaign against the Moors, who occupied a great part of Spain, when he received a packet from the king. And here the difficulty began. What did he say in those pot-hooks written on an enclosed parchment? To advance? To retreat? It was difficult to guess. The messenger had confined himself to delivering the packet and, putting spurs to his horse, disappeared in a cloud of dust.

Don Suero, perplexed, found himself with the parchment in his hand, turning it round and round, without knowing what it said. He made a man of a neighboring village come to him, a man who was an enemy of his because of a certain thrashing which he had ordered him to be given some days before, and said:

"I have been told that you know how to read and write, and as nobody else here knows how to, you will read to me what this document from the king says, and if you do not tell me the truth I will have you skinned alive. Moreover, I require from you absolute secrecy. What is said here only you and I must know."

The offended peasant promised him all, but with the idea of taking complete vengeance. And indeed hardly had he cast a glance at the document than he exclaimed in accents of the greatest surprise:

"The king orders you to give up the command of the

troops and to go immediately to the court, where you have been accused of treason."

"I a traitor! Ah, what scoundrels are those who have said that of me! I will cut off their ears with my own hand."

No sooner said than done; he at once left the command of his troops and started on his march to the court.

The journey was long and wearisome, and our Don Suero was obliged to halt in an uninhabited place, to dismount from his horse and to sleep on the blessed ground, neither more nor less than if he had been the poorest of peasants.

So he passed the night, until dawn surprised him. On collecting himself he saw a large board close to a ditch situated at the side of the road. What might that say? It ought to be something important when it was written in such large letters. He went as near as he could to see if any sign, which was not in writing, might indicate something to him of what the board said; but, alas! on going nearer he slipped and fell headlong into the ditch.

The notice said, "Take care in approaching!"

It cost him no little work to get out of it, and still the shock left him so weak that he could hardly move.

As well as he could, he approached the nearest village and got into bed. The first person whom he met was the cunning peasant who had so badly translated his majesty's letter. He was flying from Don Suero and had come face to face with him where he least expected to.

On seeing his good-natured gesture, he knew that his deceit had not been discovered, and, without trembling, he approached the noble knight.

"You can be useful to me," said the latter. "I do not feel disposed to go to the court. Write to the king what has happened to me and tell him that as soon as I am a little better I will come and confound those who have calumniated me."

But the peasant wrote what he liked and sent off the letter.

In it he heaped insults on the king, with the object of causing the latter to have the knight's head cut off.

The effect that the insulting letter produced was so great that the king rose in his anger and commanded Don Suero to be brought dead or alive, and that if he resisted he was to be tied to the tail of a horse.

The knight was imprisoned, but as he was so proud he would not give the king any explanations, and the latter commanded him to be tortured.

Not even the severest tortures could succeed in taming that will of iron. He was innocent, and would not ask grace of the king, who condemned him without any further motive. At length they were going to sentence him to death for his insults to the king, when one of the judges mentioned to the king the possibility of Don Suero having put his seal at the foot of a document he had not signed.

"Because," he said, "it is stated he does not know how to read and write."

"What!" angrily exclaimed the king. "Did I pass five long years in learning how to spell, and that silly Don Suero does not know how to do it? I do not believe it. If you cannot prove to me that the letter in which he calls me a weak and stupid king is unknown to him, I will have him killed tomorrow."

The judge did not neglect to see. He wrote out the sentence of death and took it to the prison, saying to the knight:

"Sign this and you are free!"

"What is this?"

"A writing in which you say to the king that you are innocent of what you are accused."

"If that is so, bring it and I will sign it."

And he put a cross and his seal at the foot of it.

The judge bore to the king that sentence that the prisoner had signed, believing it to be his salvation, and then the king, convinced of his innocence, commanded him to be set free and returned all his honors to him.

After that the knight dedicated himself to learning reading and writing, and made such progress that, after eight years of lessons, he already knew which was the letter O, both capital and small, which indeed showed a progress not too rapid.

And the peasant? He was sought for, being a wicked man, and as soon as he was caught he was put into prison, where he finished his life.

Ignorance is bad, but the wicked are worse than the ignorant.

THE WHITE PARROT

Once upon a time in a city in Spain a brother and sister lived with their father in a happy little home. They were especially proud of their inner courtyard which was full of rare plants. The mother was dead, and little Mariquita was mistress of the house. She was a splendid little housekeeper, and everything about the place was always bright and shining.

One day an old woman came to the door when Mariquita was at home alone. She knocked, and Mariquita ran to open the door.

"How do you do, little girl? Is your father at home?" asked the old woman.

Mariquita replied that he was away.

"Is your brother at home?" asked the old woman.

Mariquita replied that he too was away from home that day.

"What a pretty home you have!" said the old woman. "It is quite the most attractive place in the town."

Mariquita threw wide the door. "Come in and see our house," she said. "I love to show visitors about. I want you to see what a pretty courtyard we have."

The old woman admired everything about the house. When she saw the patio she said that it too was very attractive. There was only one thing that was lacking. It needed a fountain of silver water.

"I never saw a fountain of silver water," said little Mariquita. "I'd like to have one, but I don't know where I could get one."

"That is easy," said the old woman. "All you have to do is to go to a certain place with a little jar and bring home the jar full of water from the fountain you will find there. When you put it in the courtyard it will instantly become a fountain of silver water. I'll tell you exactly where to go to get it."

When Mariquita's father and brother came home they found her crying. "What is the matter?" they asked in alarm. She was such a happy little girl that they were not in the habit of seeing tears upon her cheeks.

"I want a fountain of silver water for our patio," cried Mariquita. "I'll never be happy again until I have one!"

"What nonsense!" cried her brother.

"We do not need a fountain of silver water in our patio. It is pretty enough as it is," said the father, shaking his head.

"I know just where to go to get water to make one!" cried Mariquita. "It's the easiest thing in the world to get it! I'll never be happy until I have it!"

She kept on crying until at last her brother decided to go in search of the water for her. He took a jar with him.

When he had gone a long distance he encountered a little old man, standing in the middle of the road.

"Where are you going, my lad?" asked the little old man. "Who hates you so much ast o send you into these parts?"

"I am in search of a fountain of silver water for our patio at home," replied the boy. "An old woman told my sister about it, and now my sister will never be happy again until she has one."

"There is great danger in getting this water," said the little old man thoughtfull. "You appear however to be a wise lad and perhaps will succeed. The fountain where you are going is guarded by a fierce lion. If he has his eyes closed he can see you, but if his eyes are wide open he is fast asleep. Wait carefully until you are sure his eyes are open. Then fill your jar with water and run away as fast as you can."

The lad did exactly as the little old man told him, and waited until the lion's eyes were wide open. Then he filled his water jar and hurried home with it as fast as possible.

When he emptied the jar of water in the patio, at once it changed into a lovely little fountain of silver water. Mariquita clapped her hands in joy, and even her father admitted that iwas a great ornament on the patio.

"Oh, I am so happy!" cried Mariquita. "The fountain of silver water is the loveliest thing I have ever seen!"

The next day, when her father and brother were away, the old woman came again to the door.

"I am so glad you have come!" cried Mariquita as she opened the door. "I want you to see what I have in my patio."

She led the old woman into the courtyard and showed her the fountain of silver water.

"It is a great improvement," said the old woman, "but there is something else which you need. Now you should have a little tree with leaves of silver and nuts of gold, growing beside the fountain."

"Tell me where I can get one!" cried Mariquita eagerly. "I never saw a tree with leaves of silver and nuts of gold. It must be beautiful!"

When her father and brother came home that night she told them about her visit from the old woman. There was no peace in the house until her brother had promised to start the next morning brother had promised to start the next morning in search of the tree with leaves of silver and nuts of gold.

He started early upon his journey, and after he had gone a long distance, he saw the same little old man standing in his path. He told the old man about his new quest.

"Take a horse, my lad. You'll need one, and I have one here waiting. Follow the narrow path which leads up the mountain into the forest. After you have gone for some distance in the forest you will see the tree you seek. It is guarded by a serpent, and when the serpent's head is hidden it is asleep. Wait until it is asleep, and then break off a branch from the tree. Take it home and plant it in your courtyard, and you'll soon have a tree with silver leaves and nuts of gold, just as your sister wishes."

The boy mounted the horse and followed the directions which the little old man had given him. When the serpent's head was hidden, he broke off a branch from the tree and took it home. As soon as the branch was planted in the courtyard, it grew into a lovely little tree with leaves of silver and nuts of gold.

"Oh, I am the happiest girl in the world!" cried Mariquita, when she saw it growing there beside the fountain of silver water.

All went well for many days. Then the old woman came again and knocked at the door.

"Come in and see what I have in my patio now!" cried Mariquita, opening the door.

The old woman went into the patio. " All you are lacking now is a white parrot," she said, as she looked about.

When Mariquita's father and brother came home that night, they found Mariquita once more in tears. There was no peace in the house until her brother promised to get her a white parrot.

When the lad had gone for some distance on his way, he again met the little old man. He told him about the white parrot which his sister had sent him to procure for her.

THE WHITE PARROT

"Perhaps you will be able to get this white parrot for your sister," said the little old man, "but it is a very dangerous undertaking. You will travel on and on until you come to a lovely garden, the most beautiful garden you have ever seen. You will see many wonderful birds flying about among the trees in the garden, but do not pay any attention to them. Wait a little, and you will see a white parrot, an exceedingly beautiful parrot, come and seat itself upon the round stone in the middle of the garden. It will turn slowly around, and after a while it will put its head under its wing and go to sleep. Wait until its head is under its wing and it is sound asleep before you seize it. Otherwise you will be turned into stone."

The boy followed the directions and came to a beautiful garden full of many trees with wonderful birds flying about the branches. He waited until a white parrot came flying down out of the treetops, alighting on the round stone in the center of the garden. It was the most beautiful bird he had ever seen, far lovelier than he had expected. The white parrot turned slowly round and round upon the stone, and finally it put its head under its wing. In his eagerness to obtain the beautiful bird the lad forgot to be sufficiently cautious. He seized the bird a moment too soon and was turned into stone.

Mariquita awaited her brother's return anxiously. As the days and weeks passed by and he did not come, her grief knew no bounds.

"Some evil has befallen my brother!" she cried over and over again. "It is all my fault! It was my foolish wish for a white parrot which sent him away from our happy home. Oh, why was I so foolish as to listen to the old woman?"

At last Mariquita could endure her anxiety no longer and she decided to go in search of her brother. As she went on her way she encountered a little old man in her path.

"Have you seen a lad pass by some weeks ago, a handsome lad with deep, dark eyes, and waving dark hair upon his brow?" Mariquita asked eagerly. "I am sure you would remember him if you once saw him."

The little old man replied that he knew her brother well. Then he told her of the dangers which attended the quest of the white parrot.

"I know my brother has been turned into stone!" cried Mariquita. "What shall I do? It was all my fault! It was I who sent him in search of the white parrot! Oh, why did I ever listen to the old woman who came to my door?"

"Be careful that you do not meet the same fate as your brother," said the little old man. " Now that you have gone so far on the way there is no turning back. All will be well if you do not try to seize the bird too soon."

Mariquita journeyed on and on until finally she came to the beautiful garden. She waited quietly until she saw the wonderful white parrot come flying down to the round stone in the middle of the garden. Slowly it turned around upon the stone. Then it rucked its lovely head under its snowy wing and went to sleep. The moment Mariquita stretched out her hand and seized the white parrot all the stones in the garden came to life. There was her brother standing close behind her. Her joy was unspeakable.

Mariquita and her brother invited all the stones which had been restored to human form to come home with them and celebrate the event in their house. A great feast was held which lasted for three days.

"Now that I have my own dear brother safe home again I am the happiest girl in the world! There is nothing more to

wish for!" said Mariquita. "Never again will I give way to foolish longings!"

THE CARNATION YOUTH

There was once a poor laborer who had an only daughter whom he loved very dearly. One day, when he was on his way home from his daily work, he saw a pink carnation growing beside the path. He picked it and carried it home to his daughter. She declared that it was the most beautiful carnation she had ever seen. She put it carefully into a glass of water.

That evening, as she held it in her hand, admiring it, she carelessly let it fall into the candle. The pink carnation began to burn immediately.

At that moment there suddenly appeared a handsome youth, who said to the girl sadly: "Why don't you speak to me? You will have to seek me among the rocks of the whole world." Then he disappeared as mysteriously as he had appeared.

The poor laborer's daughter had never seen such a handsome young man in her life. She dreamed of him night and day. His words kept ringing in her ears, "You will have to seek me among the rocks of the whole world."

There was nothing else for the girl to do except to go in search of the mysterious youth. She could no longer be happy in her own home. Accordingly she walked and walked.

Finally she came to a high rock on the bank of a river and as she was exceedingly tired she sat down to rest. It was very hot and she began to cry because of her great weariness and the intense heat.

Suddenly the rock opened and the handsome youth stepped out. "Why are you crying?" he asked gently.

The girl was so frightened that she could not say a word. She just kept on crying.

The handsome youth wen ton, "Over there through

the forest you will see a large house with broad fields about it. Go to the house and hire out as a servant. They will receive you gladly there." With these words he disappeared into the rock.

There was nothing better for the tired girl to do than to follow his advice, and she found the house as he had directed. The mistress of the house was in need of a maid, and she hired the girl at once. Soon the laborer's daughter became the favorite servant of the entire establishment, with her pretty face, her industrious habits, and her pleasant ways.

Then the other servants became jealous, and they plotted against her to get her into trouble. They went to their mistress and said: "Do you know what your new maid has been saying in the kitchen?"

Their mistress ordered them to tell her what it was.

"She says that you do not need to have so many servants. She alone could wash all the dirty clothes in one day."

The mistress called the little maid to her and asked if it were true. The poor girl wept and said it was false, and she had never said any such thing; but the other servants agreed that they all had heard her say it, and her mistress commanded her to wash all the dirty clothes in one day, according to her boast.

The little maid went to the river with the dirty clothes and sat down upon the rocks to cry. Suddenly the rock opened and the handsome youth stepped forth.

"Why are you crying?" he asked.

The girl was so surprised that she did not answer, but went on crying harder than ever.

The youth continued, "Do not worry about washing the clothes. Just leave them here on the river bank and ask the birds of all the world to come and help you."

The girl looked up in amazement, but the youth had disappeared into the rock.

She did as he had advised, and called out: "O birds of all the world, come and help me!"

Soon the birds of all the world came flocking to the river bank. There were big birds and little birds and middle-sized birds. There were black birds and brown birds and blue birds and red birds and yellow birds. The little maid had not known that there were so many kinds of birds in the whole world.

The birds seized the dirty garments in their beaks and shook them up and down in the river. Soon all the soiled clothes were clean and white.

In the afternoon they were dry and ready to carry home. The mistress and the other servants could not believe their eyes when they saw that the washing had all been done. The mistress loved her little maid more than ever and told all her friends what a perfect jewel of a servant she had in her employ.

Then the other servants became more jealous than ever and thought of another plot. Now it happened that their mistress had n only son who left the house one day and never came back. He had been enchanted. His poor mother wept until she nearly lost her eyesight. Accordingly, the servants went to their mistress and said that the new maid had boasted that she knew where to get an eyewater that would cure any eye trouble in the world.

Of course the poor girl had never said such a thing, but all the servants agreed that she had, and her mistress became angry because her maid had known of an eyewater which she had not obtained. Accordingly, the mistress sent the girl in search of the eyewater which would restore failing sight.

The little maid went down to the river bank and sat down upon the rocks, crying as if her heart would break. She did not know a single thing about eyewaters.

At once the rock opened and the handsome youth stepped out. "What is the matter? Why are you crying?" he asked.

As he received no reply, he went on to say, "I known how you may obtain an eyewater which will cure my mother's eyesight. Take a cup and stand by the riverbank. Then call to the birds of all the world and ask them to come and weep with you." The youth disappeared.

The little maid followed his advice and stood by the riverbank with a cup in her hands. She asked the birds of all the world to come and weep with her, and at once they came flying up to her. Each one deposited a tear in the cup and soon it was full. The last bird which came dropped a tiny white feather into the cup.

When she bathed the yes of her mistress with the water, using the tiny white feather, her mistress became better immediately. Soon she could see as well as ever, and she loved her little maid more and more.

The jealous servants plotted again against the maid. They told their mistress that she had boasted of knowing how to break the enchantment which bound the son of the house. By this time their mistress had such confidence in her maid that she believed the girl could do anything.

When she said she had never made any such boast, her mistress aid, "Never mind! Just go ahead and try! If you should succeed in breaking my son's enchantment and restoring him to me once more, I'd make you his wife."

The little maid went down to the rocks beside the river and cried as if her heart would break. The handsome youth came forth from the rock as before and asked why she was crying.

When she did not reply he said, "I know that my mother has sent you to break my enchantment. Gather together all the maidens of the town, rich and poor alike, and come and march about the rocks in a procession, each girl with a lighted candle in her hand. Be sure that no candle goes out. We'll see what that will do to break my enchantment!"

When he had once more disappeared, the little maid ran as fast as she could to gather together all the young girls of the town, rich as well as poor. A beautiful procession they made, too, when the came to march about the rocks, each with a lighted candle in her hand. The little maid was the last of all in the procession, and, just as she came to the rocks, the wind blew out her candle.

"O what shall I do! My candle has gone out!" she cried.

She saw that the handsome youth had already appeared.

"At last you have spoken in my presence!" he cried. "Now at last my enchantment is broken!"

"I thought I had spoiled everything when my candle went out!" exclaimed the little maid.

The young mane explained to her how he had been enchanted one day when he was walking in the field. He had been changed into a carnation and had been told that his enchantment would be broken only when the person who burned the carnation should speak in his presence.

"You did not say one word when you burned me," het

old her reproachfully. "I had to go back into the rocks from which the carnation had sprung, and I began to think I'd never get you to say a word to me. You didn't do anything but cry!"

The youth's mother was the happiest woman in the town when she saw that her son was restored to her, alive and well. She kissed her little maid upon both cheeks.

"You shall be my own dear daughter, now," she told her. "The wedding shall be celebrated immediately."

The little maid was entirely cured of the crying habit, and fortunate it was; for, after all the delay in getting his enchantment broken, her husband's patience could never have endured a crying woman.

For the full listing of our titles visit
www.sophenebooks.com

All of our titles are available on amazon.com, amazon.co.uk,
amazon.de, amazon.fr, amazon.es, and amazon.it